METAMORPHOSIS
GOOD GIRL GONE
BAD

By

Karen Marie
Coleman

Kaldonya Brunson
PUBLISHING

Contact Info

Email: authorkarencoleman@yahoo.com

Visit our official website at: www.karencoleman.org

Dedication

To my very special friend and dearest cousin,

"Cora D. King."

I love you dearly. Father, God placed you in my life many years ago as my best friend and guardian angel. We were inseparable. Although our destiny has taken us on different paths on our life's journey, I'll always love you and thank Father God for placing you in my life! You are one amazing lady. I love you,

Karen

Table of Contents

Chapter One

TJ honey, you've gotten all messy! Look at you." Katrina frantically looked through her purse for a wet wipe. While wiping her son down, Katrina said under her breath, "You know that woman can't stand me. She's always finding something negative to say about us," speaking of her mother-in-law. "Come here Alexis, let mommy look at you." She examined her daughter carefully.

"Mommy, I was careful not to waste anything on me!" her daughter said proudly. Katrina kissed her.

"You're a big girl, and mommy's proud of you," she said while looking them over once more. Her son was dressed in a tan suit and tie. Her daughter wore a cream-colored satin and sheer layered dress with a crystal beaded waist. Her hair was in a curly ponytail with a large satin bow that matched her dress. Pleased with her children's appearance, Katrina glanced at her reflection in the window. She was wearing a crystal-beaded, soft-yellow evening gown. Her make-up was professionally done, and so was her hair. Not a strand was out of place. She was finally ready to make her appearance. She took both children by the hand and walked into the mansion resembling a royal compound owned by her in-laws. TJ, short for Tarik Junior lagged a few steps behind his mother. She gently tugged at his arm and said, "Come on son. Keep up with Mommy."

"Mommy, why do we have to come to Grandma Frances' house? I hate her," said TJ Looking sad, he lowered his head and pulled his arm back from his mother. Katrina paused for a minute. "You shouldn't say things like that, honey. I know your Grandma Frances can be difficult, but she loves you."

"But Mommy, she's always mean to us, and she fusses all the time." Katrina leaned over and talked to both of her children. "I tell you what, if you guys are on your best behavior, Mommy will take you somewhere really special for the weekend, okay." "Can we go to the amusement park?" TJ asked. "Yes, mommy will take you if that's what you want." Both children screamed with excitement. They happily went into their grandmother's place with their mother.

Mandy, the housekeeper, greeted them at the door and escorted them inside. She announced their arrival to her in-laws. "Mrs. McAllister and the children are here," Mandy said. Mrs. Frances McAllister snapped at the housekeeper. "Mandy, how many times have I told you to call her Katrina?" The matriarch was reclining on a chaise surrounded by servers who were catering to her every demanding whim. She was dressed in a glamorous, ivory-colored evening gown draped in pearls. Her satiny grey hair fell across her chestnut, wrinkled face as she looked towards Katrina. Katrina walked inside and spoke to everyone. The staff, including Mandy, were dressed in tuxedos.

"Kids, go and give your grandmother a hug," Katrina said. She had to physically lead them over to their grandmother because neither of them went willingly. Her mother-in-law barely acknowledged them. "Happy birthday, Mother McAllister," Katrina said as she handed her mother-in-law a beautifully wrapped package inside a silk bag. She took the present Katrina had given her and tossed it aside.

As Katrina walked the children over to greet their grandfather, Mrs. McAllister asked, "Where's my son?"

"He's coming later. He had some loose ends to tie up at the office. He insisted that we come without him."

"Well, he needs to hurry. He's running late. The guests will begin arriving soon.

It was Mrs. McAllister's birthday, and she was having a lavish but quaint birthday celebration with a few of her closest friends and business partners. The city's mayor was on the guest list, as was the chief of police and the city's most prominent attorneys, judges, and businessmen. Mandy took TJ and Alexis with her as guests began arriving. Katrina excused herself to the guest bathroom. Looking in the mirror, she thought, "Lord, I'll be glad when this evening is over." Her cell phone rang. It was her husband, Tarik. "Hi honey," she said. "Your mother's asking about you. How much longer will you be?"

"I'll be on my way in a few minutes."

"Guests are arriving, and your mom insists that you be here."

"Look woman, I said I'll be on my way. I get so tired of you and your damn nagging; it's getting a little old Katrina."

"Honey, I'm sorry, I'm not trying to upset you," she said trying to calm him. "I just wanted you to know that your mother is looking for you." Katrina heard a woman's voice in the background. She recognized the voice as her husband's ex-girlfriend. She dared not ask him any questions about it. With all of her spiritual energy drained, she said, "I'll see you when you get here." She ended the call, and she sobbed a little. Katrina was suffering. She'd been suffering ever since she married Tarik. They met in college. Tarik was a spoiled momma's boy who got everything he wanted in life with the help of his parents. He never knew the meaning of the word *no*. Whenever he'd get into trouble, which was often, the McAllister money would always buy him out of it. He would commit crimes worthy of felonies but always got away with a slap on the wrist. When he made enemies, his mom would quickly buy them off. She was deeply involved in almost every aspect of his life. When he and Katrina fell in love, his mother insisted that he not marry her. From his parents' point of view, she was considered a nobody, and they felt that he could do much better than her. By then, he'd already fallen in love with her. Before their relationship, Tarik had dated Sharice Lambert. Next to the McAllister family, the Lambert's were the second wealthiest family in the state. Sharice was the girl they planned for him to marry. Her parents sent her abroad to study and pursue her interests, and she was mentored by the best in the corporate world. She branched off and opened businesses all over America and Africa for her father's company. Now she's back in Tarik's life and has been for the past year. They act as business partners, of course. Katrina knows they're sleeping together, but she dares not say anything out of fear of Tarik. The threat of his rage and physical abuse was ever-present. The first time that she asked him about the affair, he dislocated her shoulder. They've been together for almost ten years, and he's beaten her for almost nine of those. She tried reporting the abuse, but she quickly learned that no one would intervene on her behalf. Everyone was on her in-laws' payroll, and they didn't want to become enemies of the family. They're known as one of the most notorious families, and whoever challenged them quickly regretted it.

Katrina tried leaving Tarik once and even took the children with her. But he found her and coerced her into returning home. Once she was back, he beat her and locked her in the basement for a week without food. She was given water only. When he went in to check on her, she was weak and battered. It was then that he forced her to sign an agreement against her will, stating that if they were ever to divorce, he would get custody of the children. Once she signed, she was locked away for another day. She begged to see their children, but he refused. His mother came the following day to release her. While doing so, she began taunting her by reminding her that she would never get the kids or their money. She was told that she wouldn't be believed if she bothered to report them. The McAllisters had already begun portraying her as a money-hungry, conniving woman who only married their son for financial gain. She was also portrayed as unstable and an unfit mother.

People believed exactly what the McAllisters told them to believe. After having been locked up for close to a week by her husband, Mrs. McAllister escorted Katrina out of the room and helped her to shower. She had a luncheon prepared for Katrina downstairs. When she made it around the table, much to her surprise, there sat the chief of police, the county judge, and their wives. Katrina felt hopeless. They were sitting in her home while she was being abused. Mrs. McAllister, acting as if nothing had happened, welcomed Katrina to her own dining table and announced to everyone that she had been sick. Mrs. McAllister operated her son's home as if it were hers, and she came and went as she pleased. Katrina had no real say in her marriage, the lives of her children, or her own life for that matter. The McAllisters were a controlling force in her life.

A knock on the door interrupted Katrina's train of thought. "What in the hell are you doing in there so long woman? Damn, hurry your ass up and come on out of there." It was Tarik. *"How did he get here so fast?"* she thought. She looked at her watch. She'd been in there for almost fifteen minutes. She went to flush the toilet, although she hadn't used it.

"Okay, I'm coming honey," she said while wiping the tears from her eyes. She opened the door. He continued arguing. She apologized, and they went to the dinner event.

The guest had arrived, and they were about to recite their traditional birthday speeches. All of which painted Mrs. McAllister in a much fairer light than she deserved.

Tarik was among those giving his speech; Katrina stood faithfully by her husband, reluctantly agreeing with him as he recited a pretentious story on behalf of his mother. Mumbling under her breath, Katrina said,

"Dear Lord, how many more of these ass-kissing parties will I have to endure?" She was exhausted from this family and her marriage to Tarik. She endured the hardships of the relationship to remain with her

children. With her mother giving her up at an early age and no relationship with her father, she knew first-hand the pain of growing up without loving parents, and she didn't want that for her children. Her mind wandered as she tried to remember happier times with her husband. Tarik hadn't always been mean or abusive towards her. She remembered when they were in love and sharing a beautiful life. That was until his mother began interfering to the point of obsession. He wanted to please his mother and began acting aggressively towards his young wife. What started as verbal abuse soon escalated into mental and physical torment. She's been in the relationship so long that all hope of ever leaving seemed lost.

It was the mayor's time to speak. The mayor, donning a receding hairline and a toothpick in his mouth, was a sixty-year-old, three-hundred-pound, African American man around five feet. He was a former attorney and prominent businessman. He was another

McAllister puppet, and they used the mayor's office as their personal operating system. They had a say in anything that went on in the city. They would attend every council meeting and provide favors for most of the council members. They donated to each political campaign and sent money to fund their family's lavish birthdays, graduations, baby showers, and weddings. They sponsored expensive trips all in the name of political training and conferences, as research they claimed would benefit the city. When the mayor spoke, he didn't disappoint. With his pockets lined with funds from the McAllister bank accounts, he followed in the same vein as the speakers before him. He continued his praise of Mrs. McAllister, reciting how wonderful and generous she was to the city and its citizens. Her gifts included donating a recreational facility, City Park, and other buildings, all named after the McAllisters, of course.

The party went well into the night. Katrina asked to be excused so that she could take the children home. She found her husband out back, talking with some guests. As she walked towards him, his uncomfortable facial expression was apparent. She looked over his shoulder and noticed Sharice. She wasn't hard to miss due to her height of a little over six feet; she was the tallest female in the room and sought to be the best dressed. She craved attention and ensured the spotlight was always on her. She was dolled up with a lovely, bronzed complexion, a perfectly made-up face, and a full-length weave install. She wasn't nearly as beautiful as Katrina, but she had an outgoing personality and stood out from the other women. That was until Katrina entered the room. Sharice was there entertaining guests with her charm, her wit, and her gift of the gab. She acted as if she belonged there. She was raised in the lap of luxury, and her parents provided the very best for her. She attended elite schools and was well-versed in the business world. Katrina didn't know much about the family business and was intentionally kept out of the loop by her husband. She got her associate's degree in business and wanted to pursue her education further, but Tarik insisted she quit school to care for their son. She's been home ever since. Once he was of school age, she asked to further her studies but wasn't allowed to do so. Tarik's reasoning was that he wanted her to be a stay-at-home mom and raise their children herself. The tactic was simply another attempt to isolate and maintain control over her. She was, however, allowed to volunteer a couple of times a week at the homeless shelter downtown while the children were in school.

Tarik hurried over to Katrina and pulled her to the side. "What is it?" he whispered.

"I just came to let you know that I'm taking the children home to put them to bed."

"Well, I'll be home later," Tarik said. "Don't bother waiting up for me." She wanted him to leave with her, but she knew he wouldn't go, and if she asked, it would only fuel his anger. She fixed her eyes on Sharice. Sharice glanced at her but didn't acknowledge her. Katrina's sudden presence didn't threaten her, and she acted as if her coming into the room was of no real importance. When Sharice went off to college, Tarik met and married Katrina, and they started their family. Sharice resented the relationship. She thought for sure she would be the one Tarik would marry. There was a brief silence as Katrina hesitated hoping Tarik would at least see her and the children out to their vehicles. He turned towards Sharice and the guests and continued entertaining them. Katrina left. While the children slept in their seats, she drove home crying all the way. Once home, she put the children to bed and cried herself to sleep.

The alarm clock was blaring loudly in Katrina's ear. Startled, she jumped up, thinking she was late getting the children ready for school. She looked around the bedroom and noticed that Tarik never made it home. She got the children dressed and ready for school. "Where's my daddy?" Alexis asked. "He had to go to work early this morning, sweetie," Katrina told her as she put her daughter's backpack on her.

"Daddy told me he was going to take me to school today."

"He'll have to take you another time. Besides, I thought that you loved it when Mommy took you to school." Alexis smiled, "I like it when you take me to school, too, Mommy."

"Well, okay little lady, let's go! TJ, here's your lunch." They got in the car. As she was pulling down the driveway, she noticed Tarik's black Tundra coming toward them. The bright morning sun shone inside his vehicle as he approached. She could see that he was still wearing the same clothes as the previous night. A wave of sadness swept over her as she imagined her husband loving another woman. A woman he'd chosen to show kindness and respect. If only he would change his ways and treat her with the same dignity, perhaps they could make the marriage work. She felt he'd reduced her role to nothing more than a live-in nanny with whom he occasionally slept. He finally reached her car and veered his truck into her lane, blocking her path. She immediately stopped her vehicle and let down her window. Tarik yelled, "Alexis, come and get in the truck with me."

"I can take her," Katrina said.

"I promised her that I would take her to school. Come on TJ." TJ protested. "I want to ride with Mama."

"Boy, get your butt in this truck!" Tarik demanded. "Go with daddy guys." Katrina got out and helped the children into their father's vehicle. She quickly glanced at him. He didn't say anything to her, good or bad. He simply drove away. As she walked to her vehicle, she wondered when he would be home or if he would be coming home that evening. She put it out of her mind for the time being. A feeling of loneliness swept over her now that the kids were back at school. As she drove her car back to the house, she thought of her sister. After parking her car, she went back inside to give her a call.

Her sister Chandra is the younger sister by two years. Although she's younger, it's like she's older. Chandra's a devout Christian, unlike some who claim to be Christian but are lacking to some degree. She's the real thing. Katrina and Chandra share a close bond, and Katrina often confides in her sister. Katrina's not a Christian. Her sister doesn't judge her for not following her faith. They were raised in separate households. Katrina's aunt and uncle raised her because her mother was unable to care for her. Two years after Katrina was born, Chandra arrived. Katrina was raised in the country while her mother and sister lived in the big city. They saw each other at family functions, and Chandra was allowed to spend the summer months with Katrina. They spent their summers by the creek lying in the sun and dreaming of everything they would do when they got older. They made the most of the time they were allowed to spend together. They were inseparable. Not being able to communicate by phone back then, they wrote to each other constantly. This day, she needed to hear the comfort of her sister's voice. She always felt better after talking with her. Living in a world where the only people who truly loved her were her children and her sister, Chandra's encouraging words would be welcomed. Katrina let out a deep sigh when Chandra answered the phone, and she let loose. When she finished pouring her heart out, she felt as if a great weight had been lifted from her shoulders. Without fail, Chandra came through.

"Katrina, listen to me, sweetie. Whenever you're ready to leave, I'll be here for you. It may not be easy, but you'll make it. All you have to do is take the first step. Put one foot in front of the other, walk away, and don't look back."

"Chandra, it's not that simple," she explained. "When I walk away, I lose my children. Remember the contract? I can't leave my children here with them. I wouldn't know what to do."

"Katrina, we can find you a good attorney who'll help you sort things out," her sister said, trying to reassure her.

"Who's going to take the case? Nobody's willing to go up against them, and besides, where would I get the money for an attorney? They control all the money. I'm lucky he allows me to send Mom money every month, and he pays her bills. He does that to control mom. He has her so wrapped around his little finger that she'll hear nothing negative about her precious son-in-law. I used to try to tell her the truth about him, but she refused to believe me, so I quit telling her anything about him. She's blinded by the money. I want to leave, but I know they'll catch on if I try to put something back for myself. They keep track of every dime I spend. I've been trying to save a little money but it's difficult with him keeping tabs on me."

"That's okay Sis, I'm going to keep praying for you and God will tell us what we need to do."

"Okay," Katrina said not wanting to hear about God. "I tried that praying stuff, but it hasn't worked for me."

"Trust me, Sis, prayer works. We just have to be patient and let God work."

"If you say so," Katrina said. They talked until it was time for Chandra to go to work.

After talking with her sister, Katrina was in a better mood. It was nearing eleven o'clock. She decided to have her lunch on the balcony in their bedroom. She called down to the kitchen to have her lunch brought up to her. She got a magazine, went out on the balcony, and waited for her lunch. She looked out over the skyline and took in the beauty. The picturesque scene was perfect. It was a peaceful place. It's hard to believe, given all the violence that takes place there. It overlooked a small pond where the ducks gathered, and the flowers bloomed to full perfection, all seeming to compete for her attention. The trees stood proud and tall, and the grass so lush that it looked like velvet. The landscape is so beautiful that it puts the admirer in a hypnotic state of peace and tranquility. She spent her entire afternoon there. She allowed no room for negative thoughts to enter her mind. She would lie there and let her mind take her away to a perfect world that she hoped to live in one day. The kind of world she dreamt of meant no violence, only peace, safety, and happiness for herself and her children. She didn't exactly have an escape plan, but she was hopeful.

Chapter Two

Katrina's cell phone rang. It was TJ's school calling. She quickly answered. It was the school nurse. "Mrs. McAllister, I'm calling you to inform you that Tarik has broken his arm on the playground, and we need you to come quickly. We've called an ambulance, and they are on their way."

In haste, she got her purse and went to the school. She made it just in time. She talked with him as they were loading him into the ambulance. She wasn't allowed to ride with him, so she followed along behind them in her car. Once at the hospital, a cast was placed on his arm, and he was released into Katrina's care. On her way home, she called her husband. During all the excitement, she had forgotten to call him. She got no answer. After arriving at their home, she put TJ to bed and tried calling her husband again, but still no answer.

She called her mother-in-law and told her what had happened. Mrs. McAllister was able to contact Tarik, but she put her evil twist on the story, telling him that it was Katrina's fault. Tarik rushed home in anger and found Katrina in TJ's bedroom, holding him. "What in the hell did you do to my son, you bitch?"

She put TJ on the bed and stood up to brace herself for the violence she knew was coming.

"Honey, it happened at school!" Before she could get another word out, he grabbed her by her hair and began dragging her to the other room adjacent to TJ's room. He locked the door and beat and choked her unconscious. As she lay there motionless, TJ began beating on the door with his good arm, trying to get inside to help his mother. Tarik stepped out of the room and closed the door behind him, not allowing TJ to see what had happened to his mother. He walked him back to his room trying to explain to him. TJ screamed for his mother, but Tarik threatened him to be quiet or he would be next. After placing TJ back in his room, he went into the kitchen and got a glass of cold water and went back into the bedroom where Katrina was still lying unconscious. He poured the water into her face and slapped her hard. "Wake up bitch!" he said to her while slapping her face continually. Katrina began moving and moaning. He pulled her by her hair and slammed her to the bed. "Don't think you're going to get off that easy. I'm going to beat your ass until I get tired and I'm full of energy today bitch." She tried explaining to him, but it was no use. With one blow, he struck her in the face with his fist. She heard a cracking sound in her jaw. He then beat her and pulled her to the floor stomping her with so much force that his shoe came off his foot. He began kicking her so hard that he left footprints on her back and chest. He was on a higher level of anger, and he was beating her for all the frustration he was feeling within. He was beating her for questioning him the previous evening of his where-a-bouts, for business deals not going through, for traffic, for not being Sharice, and for TJ breaking his arm. She was helpless against the rage within him. He beat her continuously until he was exhausted, and she was barely hanging on. He then followed up the beating with a brief rape. Wanting to inflict mental torment on her, he asked, "Do you really want to know what I've been doing with Sharice? You keep asking about her. Well, here it is. This is what I have been doing with her; I've been giving her this dick. As he attacked her, he said, "You will never be Sharice! She'll always be a better woman than you and she'll damn sure be a better mother to my children. He ejaculated on her body and said, "You don't deserve my seed. I can't believe I got you pregnant and twice, no doubt. You can't even take care of my children properly. You let my son get hurt at that damn school, and you think that I'm going to give you more of my seed?" When he was finished, he showered and took TJ to his mother's home. Then, he went back to work as if nothing had happened. His body was sore from beating Katrina. He had an injured toe, and his fists were swollen. He was complaining about his injuries, all the while not caring about his wife, who was lying at home alone, battered and bruised.

When Katrina regained consciousness, she knew she was seriously injured. This beating was more severe than any she'd ever received at the hands of Tarik. She mustered up the strength to get to the phone. She called 911 for help, and she called her sister. She pulled her body to the door and made it to her feet. Still struggling to move, she slowly made her way downstairs and to the front door. After opening the door, she collapsed. She could barely breathe, and her ribs were sore. Her eyes were swollen shut, and her nose was swollen so bad that she had to breathe through her mouth. With each breath she took, her ribs hurt. She went unconscious again. The ambulance arrived and rushed her to the hospital. The police assumed an unknown intruder had come into the home and attacked her. Chandra arrived at the hospital. She was worried about her sister. She wasn't allowed to see her due to her grave condition. The doctors were desperately trying to save her life. She noticed a thin white man she assumed was a police detective. He was speaking with a nurse about Katrina's injuries. He was eager to speak with her so she could tell them who attacked her. After being informed of her condition, he was forced to wait until Katrina regained consciousness so that he could question her about the incident. The nurse informed him that her sister was waiting in the family area. He pulled Chandra away to ask her a few questions.

"Hi, ma'am. I'm Detective John Akers. I'm working on this case. I understand that Mrs. McAllister is your sister; is that correct?"

"Yes, she's my sister," Chandra said, with tears in her eyes.

"Do you know of anyone who would have any reason to harm Mrs. McAllister?" With her arms crossed, she said, "Why not start with that husband of hers? He's the only enemy that I know she has. Oh, but you won't investigate that because you're probably on their payroll, just like everyone else in this town. "Look ma'am, we're not going to get anywhere with you accusing anyone. I'm not the enemy here. I'm here to help find out what happened to your sister. Did she say anything to you when she called?"

"No, the only thing she said was for me to meet her at the hospital. She said she wasn't feeling well. I don't know what could've happened. Where is her husband? Have you talked with him yet?"

"Yes, after hearing about his wife's attack, he was involved in an accident a few minutes ago while coming to the hospital. He'll be arriving by ambulance," the detective told her.

"Here's my card, call me if you learn something new or if you need to talk. I'll keep you posted on our investigation."

The doctor came out about thirty minutes later to inform Chandra of Katrina's condition. "Mrs. McAllister is in a coma, due to swelling in the brain. She has a broken jaw and three cracked ribs. She's been through a lot. We are watching her closely. She has some internal bleeding, but we've managed to stop that for now. She's in critical condition in the ICU."

"Can I go back to see her?" Chandra asked.

"Yes, you can but only for a few minutes. Remember, she's still critical, and we don't want things changing for the worse." A nurse led Chandra to ICU where she was allowed to see her sister. Chandra wasn't mentally prepared for what she was about to see. As soon as she stepped into the room, the smell of medication filled the air. She noticed the EKG machine and the IV machine. She slowly looked over her sister's battered body. She was almost afraid to look at her face. Her body trembled as she focused on her face. Horrified at the sight of her sister, she burst into tears. She was unrecognizable. She had been so savagely beaten that her face was severely disfigured. Both eyes were swollen shut and bruised. Her cheeks were puffy, her nasal cavity had been intubated by doctors so she could breathe. She had a large knot on her forehead. It was apparent that a violent assault had taken place, and it appeared her attacker tried to murder her. Chandra reached for her sister's hand which was also bruised. She lightly touched her and began praying. "Katrina, I love you sissy. Hang in there for me. You can't die on me now, I need you. Your kids need you." While she was talking, Tarik walked into the room on crutches. His fists were wrapped in bandages, and he had a bandage on his forehead.

"What the hell are you doing to my wife?" He asked. Sorrow turned to anger as she heard Tarik's voice. She turned towards him with clenched fists and walked over to him. With her blood boiling over, she asked,

"What am I doing to her? The real question is what have you done to her?" Chandra got directly in his face. He could feel the heat of her breath as she spoke. His knees trembled. He could tell by the fire in her eyes she was enraged, and he was afraid she was about to become violent. He puffed his chest out and stood taller on his crutches to intimidate her. She fearlessly moved in even closer causing him to take a step backwards. "I know you did this to my sister you coward!"

"You know nothing; now I need you to leave!"

"Not everybody is afraid of you Tarik. She's my sister and I'm not leaving. I don't have to go anywhere."

"We'll see about that," Tarik said. His mouth went dry as his body continued to tremble. He looked around hoping that his mother would step in on his behalf. As abusive as he was towards his wife, he was now cowering to her younger sister. He turned his back towards her leaving her standing in the room. She comforted Katrina. He spoke with hospital personnel and had Chandra removed from the ICU. His mother was in the waiting area talking with the doctors about her condition. Chandra and Katrina's mother, Ruth Abrams, had finally arrived. She had been playing tennis with her friends and was still dressed in her tennis gear. With widened eyes, she scanned the waiting area looking for Tarik. She didn't see him, so she went to the nurse's desk where a male attendant was sitting talking on the phone. "Excuse me sir, I'm looking for my daughter Katrina McAllister."

"Yes, ma'am; the family is in the ICU waiting room. I'll have someone escort you back." She was taken back to the waiting room. The family gathered around to discuss Katrina's condition. Tarik noticed Katrina's mother, who was pacing the floor and rubbing her hands together. He made his way over to where she was standing. She looked at Tarik for answers. "What happened to my daughter?" Chandra, who had made her way back into the waiting area, said, "She was assaulted." Instead of answering her question, Tarik said,

"Ms. Ruth, your daughter's just fine, and she's going to get the best treatment money can buy. When she's stable enough, we're going to have her moved to a private hospital." He walked her away from the earshot of everyone else. "How has everything been with you? Do you need anything?"

"Ruth looked at him with a faint smile. She removed her visor from her head and took a seat. "No son; I don't need anything. Just make sure you take good care of my daughter okay."

"You know I will," he said, reassuring her. "It's about time for you to have a new vehicle, isn't it, Ms. Ruth? The one you have now is about two years old, right? You'll need something a little better to drive. When this is over, I'll need you to go down to the car lot and have them put you in anything you want. They know what to do. Here's a little something for you now, and I'm sending you a little something in the mail, okay." He kissed her on the cheek, handed her a few thousand dollars, and hobbled back over to where the rest of the family was standing.

Chandra went to her mother. "Mom, you know he's the one who hurt Katrina."

Her mother folded her arms and said in a snappy tone, "Stop saying that Chandra. You've hated that young man ever since he and your sister got married. What's your problem? Are you jealous or something?"

"Oh Mom, you have a lot to learn about people," she said in disgust.

"He's been good to Katrina and this family. He loves her and he would never allow anything to happen to her. If anything, Katrina is the one who gives him a hard time. He calls me and tells me everything she does. She doesn't have to work or anything. He takes care of everything and all she has to do is take care of his needs and their children. He says all she does is complain. She's ungrateful and spoiled and it looks to me like you're jealous of your sister."

"So, while your daughter is lying there in a coma, the only thing you can think to do is attack her. I've had enough mom. Oh, and by the way, when are you going to go back and see your daughter? You haven't stepped one foot back there, yet here you stand with a hand full of blood-money." Chandra looked at her mother in disgust. She distanced herself from everyone and prayed while keeping a close eye on Tarik. He was enjoying sympathy for a situation that he'd caused. Mrs. McAllister went to her son. "Honey, how are you feeling?"

"I'm fine, Momma."

"You know the police are asking questions about what happened to her. I told them that it had to be an intruder because you were at the office. Did you do this son?"

"Momma, she allowed my son to be hurt. What else should I have done? She was supposed to protect him. That's all I asked of her. Protect my children. She doesn't do anything but lie around the house and go shopping and volunteer at that bullshit of a homeless shelter. She cares more about those homeless people than she does her own family." His mother comforted him. "I'll take care of everything for you okay. You don't have to worry about a thing. I'll call Chief Marks at the police department, and everything will be okay."

"Okay, Mom, thanks." Tarik's cell phone rang. It was Sharice.

"Hi there," he said feeling upbeat that she'd called. She asked,

"How are you? Your mom called my dad and told him that you'd been involved in an accident. Are you okay?"

"I'll be okay when I see you. When is that going to be?"

"I'll see you as soon as I get back in town. I had to make a brief trip on my father's behalf at a business conference."

"That's my girl. You're amazing. I bet you knocked them dead."

"Absolutely. My dad's jet will be landing soon, so I'll be back in town about six hours from now."

"Baby, that's six hours too long. I need to see you right now.

I'm on my way," she told him.

"Okay call me when your plane lands."

"I will," she said.

"I need some TLC and you are the one who can do that for me."

"I'll handle that when I get there." She ended the call.

Tarik returned to where the rest of the family was standing. "Mom, I'm not feeling so well. The doctor gave me a little something for pain, and I'm going to go home and get some rest," he said.

Chandra, overhearing him, asked, "How could you leave while your wife is lying here in a coma?"

His mother stepped up and said, "Look, girl, you need to leave my son alone. He's been involved in an accident, and he needs his rest due to his injuries. He's going through a lot right now. There's nothing that he can do for Katrina by being here." She looked at Tarik. "Son, you go on home."

"Yes mother," he said. "Tell the driver to come back and get me later."

Mrs. McAllister summoned a nurse to get him a wheelchair. They wheeled him to the family car waiting outside. Mrs. McAllister looked at Ruth and said, "You guys have nothing to worry about. When Katrina is stabilized, we will have her moved to a private hospital."

"Thank you, Mrs. McAllister. I don't know how I could ever thank you for all you do for my daughter." Mrs. McAllister patted Ruth on the shoulder and they walked away from Chandra and talked a while. Chandra pulled out the card that the detective had given her earlier and gave him a call. He answered.

"Hello, Detective Akers."

"Hello Ma'am" "Detective, this is Chandra Abrams. We met at the hospital a little while ago about my sister Katrina McAllister."

"Yes Ms. Abrams, how may I help you?"

"I wanted to know exactly what you're doing to bring my sister's attacker to justice?"

"Ms. Abrams, we're still working on the case. I'm at her home now. We're gathering as much evidence as we can and we're doing everything to piece together what happened and who could've done this to her."

"What have you guys come up with so far? Does it look like an intruder because I have a strong suspicion that her husband did this to her?"

"Ma'am, we don't know anything at this time. I understand your concern for your sister, but for now, let's keep your accusations at a minimum."

"Look, Detective, my sister often confides in me about his constant abuse. I've advised her to leave but she stays with him for the sake of her children. I believe he did this to my sister. I wish you guys would hurry and find something because we need to know the truth and put this abuser behind bars for good this time. He abuses my sister often, yet you guys never seem to arrest him, even after she filed a complaint against him."

"Ma'am, do you have any proof of him abusing her? Do you have any proof that he has done this to your sister? If not, then I suggest you leave the police work to me and allow me to do my job, and I'll do my best to bring whoever committed this crime to justice."

"I bet you will," she said sarcastically. Out of frustration, she ended the call. She cried softly to herself, and she continued praying for her sister.

Detective John Akers really was gathering evidence, and he was actively trying to get to the bottom of what happened. He wasn't on the McAllister's payroll. He's an officer of integrity, and he keeps to himself. He's been on the force for twenty-seven years and is looking to retire in about seven years. He's a good detective and solves a huge percentage of his cases. He is very meticulous, and he rarely misses any details regarding his cases. He walked up to the bedroom where the incident took place. There was broken furniture, and the room was in disarray. He was looking for evidence of an intruder. He noticed there were no signs of forced entry. Whoever attacked Katrina knew her. Her attacker was allowed to come all the way upstairs. He spoke to a colleague, Detective Robert Billings, who was also going over the crime scene with him. "Billings, she knew her attacker. There's no sign of forced entry."

"Could've been a repairman or someone like that," said Billings.

"I'm going to keep looking around here. In the meantime, check with her husband and see who all had access to the home." The forensics team came to process the scene. Photos were taken of everything in the bedroom. Detective Akers noticed fresh stains and blood on the sheets. He demanded that all evidence be taken to the crime lab for further analysis. As customary, he'd also requested a rape kit to be administered to Katrina as well as hair and fingernail samples. They were almost done processing the place when Tarik came in. The detectives questioned him, but he was slick and hid behind his injuries. He asked if they could process what they could and leave. After a couple of hours, they were finished.

"We'll be in touch," Detective Akers said. "If there's anything that we can do for you and your family, let us know," said Detective Billings. Tarik tried to show concern for his wife. As far as the detectives could tell, he was an asshole, but that didn't make him guilty. The detectives left, and Tarik looked in the bedroom to see what had been taken by the detectives. He noticed the sheets and bedspread missing. He called his mother and told her what had been taken. He didn't care about his DNA being on the sheets because it was his home, and he already had an answer for anyone who would question why it was there. Nobody saw the attack, and it just so happened that their housekeeper was out running errands, so she wasn't a witness. She was unaware that Tarik had come home that day, and even if she had been there, she would've known to keep her mouth closed out of fear for her job and the McAllisters. Nobody crossed the McAllisters without paying a steep price. Tarik ordered her to clean up the bedroom, and he went into the den to wait for Sharice's call.

Chapter Three

Chandra spent the night at the hospital. She wanted to be the first person Katrina saw when she came out of her coma. There was still no change in her condition. Chandra thought of her niece and nephew. She wanted to speak with them and perhaps comfort them during this difficult time, but she knew Tarik wouldn't allow it. She rarely got to visit with them due to Tarik's isolation from Katrina, so she was only able to see them when Katrina went to visit their mother. When she was alone with the children, she allowed them to call her. Tarik didn't allow too many visits from Chandra to their home. He only approved of Katrina seeing her mother but monopolized her time in such a way that she couldn't do much else. Unbeknownst to him, Chandra would stop by and have lunch with Katrina at the homeless shelter where she volunteered. It was their secret. Tarik and his mother finally arrived at the hospital, expressing concern for Katrina. The doctors ingratiated themselves to them by sharing all the details of Katrina's condition. Chandra was treated like an outsider. When she asked about her sister, no one would give her any information, citing privacy laws. As soon as the McAllisters' arrived, they were given a complete, detailed description of her status. She moved closer to hear what the doctors were saying to them. "Mrs. McAllister's brain swelling has gone down some. She's still in a coma. All we can do at this point is pray she comes out of it. She's stable, and the helicopter will be here soon to take her to the Westwind Medical facility, as you requested. They're the best, and they'll take good care of her. As you know, that's where our governor was treated when he had his skiing accident. She'll get one-on-one care and have a personal team of doctors and nurses around the clock devoted only to her," the doctor said.

Frustrated with what she was hearing, Chandra said, "I don't believe it! You guys are moving my sister? How could you?"

Mrs. McAllister spoke up. "It's for the best. She'll get the best care that money can buy. Didn't you just hear the doctor? Even he knows this is what's best for her. We love Katrina and we're doing the right thing. I'm sorry you're upset but it's not your decision. She's Tarik's wife, and he can do as he pleases. If he wants his wife to get the best care, then who are you to tell him he can't make sure that happens?" Chandra couldn't speak. She ran back into the hospital room where her sister lay. She laid her head on her chest and sobbed. She lay there until the nurses came and escorted her away. Chandra went home devastated.

Med flight arrived and took Katrina to Westwind Medical Center. As the family was leaving the hospital, Detective Akers called Tarik.

"Hi, Mr. McAllister, Detective John Akers here. I'd like to talk with you. I'd like to know if you could stop by the station. I have a few things I would like to discuss with you and clear up a few things. When can you come by?"

"I'm afraid I can't. You're going to have to talk to me by phone."

"I can come by your home if you can't make it to the station," said Detective Akers.

"You can talk to me now. Exactly what is it that you need to discuss with me?"

"I'd rather talk with you in person," he told him.

"Well, that's not going to be any time soon, so it looks like you'll have to wait. Now is not the right time because we're having my wife moved to a better facility. Perhaps you can call me in a few weeks." Tarik ended the phone call and told his mother. She immediately got on the phone and called the chief of police. He was unavailable, but she left him a message. When they arrived at Tarik's home, Detective Akers was already there waiting for them. Tarik got in the face and said,

"I thought I told you that this is not a good time."

"Don't you want an update on your wife's case?"

"Of course I do, but we could've discussed it by phone."

"Mr. McAllister, I have to take you downtown for a more thorough interview."

"Why?" Mrs. McAllister moved in between the two men. She slightly pushed Tarik out of the way and said,

"You're not taking my son anywhere. You need to speak with our attorney if you have any more questions. Now, do you have a warrant? If not, then I suggest you leave this property right now, or else I'll slap you with a lawsuit so harsh your great-grandchildren will feel the effects." She got in his face. "And who in the hell do you think you are, coming on private property without a warrant demanding to take my son off this property? I think it's in your best interest to leave."

Detective Akers said, "Ma'am, this is an official crime scene, and I have every right to be here. I'm not accusing him of a crime, and I want to speak with him to assist in our investigation. Perhaps he can shed some light on a few issues that have us puzzled. If he's innocent, then he has nothing to worry about. Let him come down to the station and talk to us."

"What do you mean, *"If he's innocent?"* Of course, he's innocent, and you don't have any evidence to suggest otherwise? He told you that you could talk to him by phone. You wouldn't accept that, so now you can talk to our attorney."

"Detective Akers said, "With the evidence that we've collected at the scene, we just wanted to exclude Mr. McAllister. I'm not saying he's a suspect; I only wanted to get a sample of his DNA so that we can clear him and catch the person who did this to your daughter-in-law."

"Our attorney will contact you," Mrs. McAllister said.

Tarik said confidently, "I'll give you a sample of my DNA., but you know that my DNA is all over that room because I live here. Mom, let's go ahead and go to the station with him. We'll follow you," he told the detective. When they arrived at the station, photos were taken of Tarik and his injuries; also, a sample of his DNA was taken. After they left, Detective Akers turned to Detective Billings and asked,

"Isn't it odd that both his fists were injured in a car accident, but there are no real injuries to the rest of his body? Mrs. McAllister has footprints on her back and chest and is in a coma from her injuries. He's hopping along on crutches with injuries to his right foot. What are the chances that he did this to his wife?

"I'm not sure; perhaps when his wife regains consciousness, she can tell us. Other than that, we'll have to wait. He's right, though. He lives there, so his DNA will be there. What happened to the rape kit that was performed on her?"

"You'll have to call Stephanie in the lab about the results on that one," said Billings. After Detective Akers got the results of the rape evidence, it was noted that Tarik's semen was present on Katrina's body and the bedding. Given what Chandra told him about Tarik's abuse of Katrina, he knew that Tarik had been the sole perpetrator of his wife. He was about to obtain an arrest warrant for him when the Chief of police called him into his office. "Chief, you asked to see me?"

"The chief, a thin Caucasian man with a receding hairline, leaned back in his chair and said, yes, I did. Akers, I'm reassigning you to the Jackson case. I'm letting Billings take over the McAllister case. I could really use you on the Jackson case." Confused, Detective Akers said,

"Chief, you can't take me off this case. I was just about to wrap it up."

"We'll let Billings take care of that. You have been reassigned, so give him your case files and move on to the Jackson case." Detective Akers did as he was told. Suspicious about his sudden reassignment and knowing the McAllisters and the Chief were close friends, he secretly made copies of all his findings before handing the case to Detective Billings. He put them away for safekeeping at his home. When Chandra called, he informed her that he had been reassigned but that they had all but solved the case and that an arrest could be made soon. He gave her the number of the proper authorities to contact about the case.

Chief Marks called Mrs. McAllister. "I've taken care of everything for you. You'll have no more problems out of this department." He reassured her. The chief asked, "How's Frank doing?"

"He's doing well. He went on a business trip," she said.

"Have him call me. I have a golf trip planned for us in Augusta, Georgia."

"You can call him yourself in about two hours. He'll be available then."

"Okay," Chief Marks said. They said their goodbyes and ended their call.

After being in the hospital for a couple of weeks, the swelling in her brain had gone completely down, and Katrina was out of the coma but was still unable to care for herself. She was on a feeding tube due to her broken jaw that had been wired shut. She was unable to perform basic human functions. She was released from the facility into the care of her husband, who had a hospital-style room set up in the east part of their home. Her physicians suggested that she be at home in her own environment to ensure a speedy recovery.

The family hired three private nurses. A rehab coach named Mrs. Jane Wheatley was assigned to the family to get Katrina back to normal. She was the best physical therapist in her field, and she came highly recommended. In the beginning, Katrina was unable to do anything for herself, but within weeks,

Mrs. Jane worked with her, getting her body used to moving again. Katrina was getting better with the help of her rehab coach. Slowly progressing, she began sitting up on her own, and most of her physical abilities were returning. All the while, Tarik came and went. He rarely spent time in their home. He was either working or spending time with Sharice. He never took the time to notice how his wife was progressing. The children were living at his parent's home. Mandy brought the children by to see their mother often.

It was in Katrina's second month of rehab that she began to walk on her own. The feeding tube had been removed, and she was able to sip liquids and food that had been processed for her consumption while the wire was still in place. By the third month, she was almost back to normal. Mrs. Jane walked with her daily around the family home and on the treadmill. Soon, Mrs. Jane began taking her out to a nearby park where she would walk Katrina around the track. Chandra would secretly meet her every day and talk with her. They never let Mrs. Jane know that they were related to ensure that she wouldn't tell Tarik. By her fourth month, her children moved back home, and her life was returning to its normal pace. She was still in a fragile state. Tarik began spending more time at home only to keep Katrina and the children under his control making them aware that he was still in control. Although Katrina was much better, she was experiencing severe headaches. She accepted that they would be a part of her world and was placed on strong pain meds. Fully aware of what had happened to her, she refused to tell her family or the police that her husband was the one who had attacked her. She would say or do just about anything to remain with her children, even if that meant keeping quiet about the abuse. She told anyone who asked that she had no recollection of the attack. She knew that even if she told, nothing would happen to Tarik. Her in-laws would make sure of that. Mrs. Jane was still coming by. She and Katrina had become quite close. When she was around, Tarik would be on his best behavior. Katrina would do everything in her power to keep Mrs. Jane around for as long as she could. Mrs. Jane was wise about many things and would share that wisdom with Katrina. They enjoyed nice long talks. She was a welcome balance in Katrina's unbalanced world. Alexis, TJ, Chandra, and Mrs. Jane were all instrumental in keeping her going.

Katrina's rehab session had ended for the day, and she walked Mrs. Jane to her car. As they were talking, Tarik overheard them. He could tell that they had become close. Almost too close for him.

Hugging Mrs. Jane goodbye, Katrina said, "I don't know what I would do without you. I wish I could keep you around. I just hate when you have to leave Mrs. Jane."

"So do I sweetheart. I've become fond of you and the children. You guys have made me feel so welcome here. I love working with you. I feel guilty that you guys pay me because I enjoy being around you. Pretty soon, you won't need me anymore. You're doing so well. I've never seen a patient do as well as you, given your severe injuries," Mrs. Jane told her.

"It was because of your patience with me. In the beginning, it was tough. I didn't think I would make it, but thanks to you, I'm much better. Do you think that when I'm done with my rehab, you can continue to come by for a visit and have dinner with us from time to time? The children and I would love that. When you're around, the atmosphere here is much more pleasant and less stressful."

"Of course I will, sweetheart. I'd love to."

Katrina gave Mrs. Jane another hug and she got in her car and left. She stood still watching her car as she pulled from the driveway wishing she could go with her. She reluctantly turned around to go back inside. As she was walking towards the doorway, Tarik came out. He took her by the hand and walked her towards the foyer.

"I think that Mrs. Jane has done a wonderful job with you, Honey."

Katrina, not wanting to look Tarik in the eyes, said, "Yes, she has." She's been a great help physically and mentally."

"You're doing so well. We won't need her around anymore. She's done what we hired her to do. Her job is professional, and she doesn't need to get personally attached to you. I don't believe it's in your best interest that she be allowed to continue coming around. I think her presence here is beginning to handicap you, and I fear that you've become far too dependent on her. You're starting to get a little lazy. I mean, she's a sweet woman, but her services would be better served by someone who truly needs her. I know you're fond of her, but the relationship that you two have is unhealthy. She's an employee, and you never want to cross that line. I'll call her supervisors and let them know that her services here are no longer needed. Don't worry; I'll see to it that she is handsomely rewarded for the great job that she's done with you. Now, you need to focus more on this family and our needs. Your children need their mother, and I need you to care for them. I'll be putting in more hours at the office. We're working on this multimillion-dollar merger, and I don't need some stranger here with my family while I'm gone. The only way that you're going to be okay is to begin to do things on your own with my children." Katrina was heartbroken, but Tarik's mind was made up concerning Mrs. Jane.

He kissed her on the cheek and left. Katrina went to the children's play area and sat while they played.

Although she was there with her children, she felt a sense of sadness and despair. She was going to miss Mrs. Jane. The thought of never being able to see her was disheartening. She played with her children the rest of the evening until the housekeeper called and informed her that dinner was ready. After dinner, she put the children to bed, showered, and called Chandra. Tarik never came home that night. Things were returning to normal and the thought of it all was depressing to Katrina. Due to her injuries, she's been experiencing constant pain in her body, including headaches. The physical pain was bad, but the constant nagging and emotional trauma was sheer torment, all from a man who once claimed to love her.

Katrina loved Tarik, but the results of his constant abuse created bitterness deep within, causing her to lose all desire for him. Before the attack, she'd reasoned within, thinking, "If he would stop the abuse, the infidelity, and begin to think for himself and not live under the shadow of his parents, she felt that she would desire him again. But she's gone through so much in the past that she no longer feels the same about the relationship. She simply wants to leave with her children. He's allowed to live his life to the fullest while she was unable to enjoy even the simplest of things. A prisoner in her own home, he holds her hostage by using the children as bait, with the threat that if she ever left, he would take them for good. It's the only reason she hasn't left him. She would've been gone long ago if they didn't have children together. She felt sorry for him. Initially, he was a better person than his parents, but his choice to walk in their path created a bad-boy persona that gave him so-called respect among his friends and admirers among women.

Tarik thinks of Katrina as his personal property, and he's unwilling to let her go. She's just another trophy among his many accomplishments. She was incredibly beautiful, and she had many suitors while they were in college. She was one of the most beautiful girls on campus. Sharice was the richest, but Katrina was more beautiful. She was also more popular even in high school. She was an honors student throughout her school years and the valedictorian at her high school. She was awarded a full-ride scholarship from the Sloane Corporation. When Sharice, who was Tarik's girlfriend at the time, left for college, Tarik set his sights on Katrina. She was the prize to behold. She was on his radar, and he had to have her. His admiration for her turned into pure obsession. Wanting to impress her, he did everything he could to get her to notice him. He sent letters, flowers, and lavish gifts, but she returned them all. She was more into her studies and wasn't interested in spoiled rich college boys in the least. She was annoyed by their snobby attitudes, wild parties, and lifestyles. Once, Tarik threw a party on his family's yacht and invited her. Against her better judgment, she decided to go so that perhaps she could convince him to stop bothering her. Much to his surprise, she accepted the invitation. Excited that she decided to come, he entertained her all night while ignoring his other guests. He was on his best behavior. He was smitten with her. He went out of his way to ensure her happiness. She didn't think she would enjoy herself. She was glad she'd cleared her schedule long enough to enjoy some brief fun. She was still uninterested in dating Tarik. After the party, she went back to her world, and it was expected that he would go back to his. He pursued her even more. Most girls fell at his feet. He was used to that, but not Katrina. She was her own woman, strong and beautiful. She was sure of herself and she needed no one's approval. Wanting to further her career opportunities, she needed no distractions from a spoiled rich kid who was looking for his latest conquest. She wasn't about to be another sex kitten trophy of his or another notch in his belt that he could brag about campus to his friends. She had invested too much in her schooling. She had no rich parents to fall back on, and she sought to make the most of a wonderful opportunity that was handed to her by a kind businessman interested in African American young ladies succeeding.

She was raised in a small town and she enjoyed the simpler things in life. She and Tarik were from two different worlds. Even so, he was in constant pursuit of her. The more she spurned his advances, the more driven he became, constantly pursuing her without fail. He began taking classes with her, hanging out in her circle of friends, going places that she liked, and getting involved in the activities that meant the most to her. She volunteered at the local homeless shelter, and Tarik would go to assist her once a week.

He even had his parents donate money to the shelter on her behalf. After a while, she thought that perhaps he wasn't so bad and that she was being too strict on him and her own love life, so they began dating. Soon, they were in love and planned to marry. When Tarik announced their engagement to his parents, they were devastated. They'd set their sights on Sharice as a suitable mate for him.

Katrina wasn't who they wanted for their son. She wasn't rich. They felt that Tarik had a lot to lose by marrying a girl who didn't have money, and by doing so, he was jeopardizing the family's finances. If the marriage failed, they could lose millions to a woman undeserved. Marrying Sharice was more beneficial for them. Tarik went against his parents' wishes and married Katrina anyway. His mother harassed him constantly about the marriage. She hated Katrina and wasn't shy about letting him know how she felt. Katrina tried staying away from her in-laws as much as possible but there was no escape from the smothering family. Mrs. McAllister was overbearing and immediately inserted herself into every aspect of their lives. Tarik was torn between pleasing his mother or his new bride. He wanted all the nagging from his mother to stop, especially with constant talks of cutting him off from the family's finances so he began giving in to his mother's demands. The pressure began to take its toll, and little by little, he began acting out in rage toward Katrina. It began with verbal abuse, occasionally slapping her, and escalated into full-blown assaults. She fought back in the beginning. The more she fought, the worse the abuse got. She then felt that if she complied with his demands and pleased him, perhaps he would back off. Nothing she tried seemed to calm him. After the birth of her children and his constant threats of denying her custody, if she were to leave, he had a broken spirit, and so she settled.

Chapter Four

Katrina's headaches were getting worse. Her doctor increased the dosage of her pain medication. She was given oxycodone. It helped but it often left her drowsy and unable to properly care for herself or her children. She tried monitoring how she took the medicine by only taking it while the children were at school or bedtime. In the meantime, she tried to live as much of a normal life as possible. Alexis' fifth birthday was coming up the following weekend, and Katrina planned a lavish party. She had been planning it for weeks. Nothing was too good for her daughter. Planning the party lifted her spirits, and she looked forward to the event. Finally, Friday came, the day before the party was to begin. She was exhausted from all the work she had put in and she had overexerted herself. The stress of the party being a success sent her into a pain frenzy. It was severe, but she refused to take any pain meds because she was taking her daughter shopping that day. Katrina kept Alexis away from the home because of the many deliveries that were being made and set up for her party. Katrina set up a petting zoo, and her favorite television characters, clowns, and a few amusement park-style rides were ordered. It was to resemble a carnival-type atmosphere. When all was done, Katrina had spent close to seventy-five thousand dollars. To the McAllisters' it was more like spending a few dollars. It was a mere drop in the bucket. This was fitting and the McAllisters agreed to this because their name was attached to the party. Most of the children that had been invited were the children and grandchildren of their closest associates.

Alexis was excited the entire day. Katrina took short breaks due to her headaches to make it through the day. TJ was with his dad. It was getting dark by the time they all made it home. Alexis was so excited about the following day that she hardly got any sleep, keeping Katrina up most of the night with her. She finally went to sleep around three in the morning. Katrina tried to get a little sleep before the long day ahead.

Alexis woke early, ran into her parents' bedroom, and climbed onto the bed. Jumping up and down in her parent's bed, she yelled in excitement, "Mommy, Daddy, wake up. It's my birthday!" Tarik turned over. He was irritated about what was happening. He looked at Katrina and said, "Katrina, get her."

She sat up in bed. "Yes baby, it's your birthday. Come on, let's go and get you ready for breakfast."

Katrina got out of bed quickly, and the blood rushed to her head. In an instant, pain shot to her brain rapidly, and she was forced to sit back down. All the while, Alexis was still yelling and singing about her birthday, further irritating her father. Tarik yelled at Katrina. "Get her out of here so I can get some rest!" Katrina grabbed her head and almost fainted due to the pain. By then, Tarik was getting out of bed in anger. He stormed into their bathroom, arguing with Katrina on the way. She managed to get Alexis and took her to her room. Her headache was so severe she knew she had to take her pain meds, or she would not be able to make it through the day. After bathing Alexis and TJ, she took them downstairs for breakfast. She got a glass of water and took her pill. The caterers and vendors began showing up to continue setting up the place. They brought in the animals for the petting zoo. Gifts were showing up from all over the US from McAllister's business clientele. The place was as busy as Grand Central. The doorbell rang nonstop. Trucks were coming and going. It was getting close to the time for the visitors to arrive and Katrina took Alexis to change into her birthday clothes. She took another painkiller and went out back to the party. When Alexis saw all that her mother had done, she screamed with excitement.

They hired videographers and professional photographers. Tarik and his parents were there. Katrina's mom stopped by briefly, but she didn't stay long. Close to eighty children and around seventy parents were present. Out of all the invitations sent, no one canceled for fear of being blacklisted by the family. For most of them, it would've been a costly mistake had they not made an appearance and made sure to sign the guestbook. It was certain that they would be severed from any future business endeavors. Katrina had a small, extravagant menu prepared for the adults and a place where they could dine while their children enjoyed themselves. Party aides were hired to help with the children. Katrina was getting drowsy from the effects of her pain meds. She was nervous about it, but she continued. It was time to cut the cake, so everyone was corralled together to sing the birthday song. After that, Alexis was allowed to open a few presents, and the children ate and played until sundown. Katrina was way past the point of severe exhaustion and was very drowsy. She went into the area where Tarik and his parents were. She was feeling awful. As she walked into the room, she fell to the floor in front of the guests. Tarik, more embarrassed than caring about his wife, went to help her. She had already made it to her feet. It appeared to them that she had had too much to drink, but she was suffering from lack of sleep and the effects of the medication. Tarik helped her to their bedroom as the guest showed concern for her. Once in the bedroom, he slammed her to the bed in rage. He crawled over the top of her, straddling her, and asked her in a whisper, "What the fuck is wrong with you, woman? You just had to show your ass here today, didn't you? Here you are, embarrassing yourself and this family in front of all these people. She tried to speak, but he took his hand and firmly placed it over her mouth and whispered, "As soon as these guests leave, I'm going to beat your ass, do you hear me?"

Katrina, too tired and not caring anymore, said to him, "Why wait? Go ahead and do it now."

After a hard slap to her cheek, he grabbed his revolver from the nightstand and put it in her mouth. "I will kill you right now bitch! Don't you ever get smart with me again? I don't give a damn about those people out there. I will blow your fucking head off. Do you hear me bitch?"

Katrina's body shook uncontrollably. Her mouth went dry as her life flashed before her eyes.

Tarik had always hit her, but he had never pulled a gun on her. This was a new low, even for him, and looking at the evil glare in his eyes, she knew that she would die on this evening. He slapped her around a few more times and forced her to sit up. He walked to the door and cracked it a little to ensure he didn't have an unwanted audience.

Katrina asked, "Why don't you just let me leave? You don't love me anymore. You and Sharice can enjoy your lives together. Just let me take care of my children. I promise I won't bother you or seek any support. Just let us go."

"Bitch, you will never step one foot out of this house with my children." He continued to berate her.

"She said, "Well, if I can't have my children, then I would rather you kill me right now. I'm already a dead woman." She stood to her feet and walked towards him. At that, he placed the gun to her head. His mother walked into the room. She saw what was taking place. With a grim smile, she said, "Not now, son. There are too many witnesses." Katrina looked at her mother-in-law in total disgust and said, "You would consent to him killing his children's mother, wouldn't you? You guys have done enough. I'm taking my children, and I'm leaving." She knew she wouldn't make it out alive. She was prompting him to make the next move. If he didn't shoot her, she would take her children and leave.

He knocked her to the floor with a backhand. His mother went in to speak with the guests, telling them that Katrina had fallen ill and that the doctor was on his way. She encouraged the guest to gather their children and leave. She closed the party down, and it took only twenty minutes for the guests to clear out. Tarik locked himself and Katrina in the room for the next couple of hours while his mother saw to it that the vendors gathered their things and left. His dad helped to escort everyone from the premises. He took the children back to the McAllister mansion. After returning to the room with Tarik and Katrina, his mother asked him, "So what do you want to do with her son? I'm about sick of this woman. It's time for you to make a decision. Whatever you decide, I'm behind you one hundred percent. Whatever happens, she leaves today. Whether in a body bag or divorce, I want her out of our lives permanently. She's been nothing but a liability since we've known her. She must go now!"

"Well, let's ask her what she wants." He placed the barrel of the gun under Katrina's chin, lifted her head with it, and asked, "Honey, what do you think I should do?" Katrina was fearful of what would happen to her children if Tarik pulled the trigger. With all that she had suffered at the hands of this family over the years, dying would be a welcome event. But her children needed her, and she needed them, and she knew that she couldn't help them if she was dead. So, rather than provoking them any further, she spoke out.

"Just let me go. I won't bother you all again. If you let me leave, you'll never hear from me. I won't ask for anything, and I will never petition the court for custody of the children."

"Mrs. McAllister said to her, "Oh, that's not a real threat to us, dear. Don't you know that I have every judge and attorney in my pocket? I pay them a handsome salary on top of what they already make. This town is mine from the Mayor down to the street cop. So, what can you do to hurt this family? Not a damn thing. So, you see, my dear, we could kill you right now, and they would come and mop up your miserable, measly ass, and no one would even bat an eye or investigate. You're worthless. You're nothing; nobody loves you, least of all this family. Why your own fucking mother sells you out all the time. She's even on our payroll. She can't wipe her ass without this family. We've had her in the palm of our hands since this sham of a marriage took place. You only married my son for the money, tricking him into marrying you without a prenuptial agreement. Hell son, why don't we just get rid of her and her whole damn family, especially that nosey-assed, pushy sister of hers. Chief Marks told me how she kept calling down there, harassing the department while she was in the hospital. They're nothing but meddling whores, the whole family." Katrina begged for her life, especially when she began threatening to harm Chandra. While she was pleading for her life, Mrs. McAllister pushed Tarik out of the way, and placed her hands around Katrina's throat, and asked, "Give me one reason why we shouldn't kill you right now?"

Katrina said, "What would you tell the children? How will you look them in their faces and tell them what happened to their mother? How can you two look at Alexis and tell her that her mother was killed on her birthday by her grandmother and her father?" Neither Tarik nor his mother answered. Mrs. McAllister tightened her grip on Katrina's throat briefly, and then she loosened it.

"We'll allow you to leave here with the clothes on your back. If you ever come around here or bother this family again, we'll come after you and your entire family. When all is said and done, there is no telling who will get hurt. Do you understand?"

Katrina nodded her head yes. She removed her hands from her neck and let her up. You can take that little piece-of-shit car with you. That's our gift to you so that you can get the hell away from this family as soon as possible. Get your purse and leave." Katrina hurried to her feet as fast as she could, with Tarik still pointing the gun at her, and watched as she got her purse. Mrs. McAllister went downstairs to fix herself a drink and sat on the sofa. Tarik marched Katrina down the stairs and towards the door. She ran to her car and drove away.

Distraught, she called her sister and asked if she could come over without telling her what happened. Chandra knew something had gone terribly wrong. She met her at the door with open arms. Katrina fell in her arms while crying uncontrollably. Chandra walked her to the sofa and held her. She didn't pressure her. She simply allowed her time to grieve. Katrina cried all night, and Chandra sat with her and silently prayed for her. Katrina finally cried herself to sleep. When morning came, she asked her sister, "Can I crash here for a while?"

"Of course, you can. You can live here as long as you like." Chandra fixed the spare bedroom for her. Katrina went and climbed into bed and didn't leave the bed all day except to use the restroom. She wasn't eating or sleeping. She stayed inside crying for a couple of days. Chandra would go in and check on her and leave her food and drink, but Katrina refused to eat. After about four days, Chandra went in and tried to coax her into taking a little chicken broth. She knew she would become very sick. Katrina agreed to drink the broth, and afterward, she took her pain meds and went to sleep. She settled into deep despair while holed up in the room for another week. Finally, she came out to shower. She borrowed some clothes from her sister. She still wasn't in the mood to eat, but she drank fruit juice while taking her meds. She began to run out, so she made an appointment to see her doctor. Once there, she was informed that she was no longer covered by the McAllisters' insurance. He treated her anyway and gave her one more prescription. She got it filled, and she went to the bank.

Her name had been taken off all the accounts, and the only money that she had was a few hundred dollars in one account given to her by Tarik, with around five hundred dollars in cash left in her purse. She stopped by the store, got herself a bottle of Cabernet, and returned to Chandra's place. She took her pill and drank a glass of wine. She went into the living room and turned on the television. Chandra came in and sat next to her on the sofa. Katrina was mellow and feeling a little zoned out. She was ready to discuss what happened between her and Tarik.

She told her sister everything that she had gone through over the years. She even revealed the truth about the recent attack in which Tarik had put her in a coma and the latest attack in which he and his mother threatened to kill her and her family. Chandra could hardly believe what she heard but knew her sister was telling the truth. Katrina had been telling her about the abuse that she suffered, but she never told her sister how severe it was. Katrina made her promise not to intervene for her safety and that of her children. Chandra was heartbroken over her sister's story. She was furious, but she knew there was nothing she could do. She continued to pray for her. In the meantime, Katrina was still having medical issues, and with no insurance, she was forced to go to the county hospital for treatment, where her new doctor limited her dosage. She tried to cope with the pain as best she could. She was in financial turmoil, and she couldn't get a job due to the severe headaches. She began drinking more, and she became addicted to the pain meds. One Friday evening, she went out to clear her head. She met a young lady by the name of René. She was a longtime patron of the nightclub. She was a beautiful young lady. She was about five feet tall and weighed under one hundred fifty pounds. She had coal-black silky hair. She was happy and upbeat. She was outgoing and had a fun personality, so when she noticed Katrina sitting alone and looking sad, she went over and made small talk with her.

"Hi, there! Things can't be that bad, can they?" Katrina smiled and said, "If you only knew."

"Well, cheer up; things can only get better. What are you drinking?"

"Cabernet"

She ordered a glass of wine for Katrina and herself. They sat and drank and continued to chat a little. Katrina found herself sharing a few details about her bad marriage. She told her about the headaches and other hardships. Before long, Rene had managed to lift her spirit. Katrina loosened up, and they went to the dance floor. Several of the young guys noticed them and danced with them. Katrina danced herself into a frenzy. She and René were back and forth from the bar to the dance floor. The young men were buying their drinks all evening. The girls went to the restroom together. Feeling a headache coming on, Katrina leaned against the wall and fumbled through her purse, looking for her meds. Rene saw what was happening.

"What's wrong girl?"

"Trying to find my headache pills,"

"What are you taking?"

"Oxycodone," she told her.

"Here, try some of this." Rene got her keychain and unscrewed the top to a little vial. She got the tiny spoon, put it to Katrina's nose, and told her to sniff.

"I don't know about that," Katrina said.

"It'll make you feel better. It'll rid you of those headaches. I promise." Katrina did as she suggested and took a deep whiff. Rene inserted the spoon back into the bottle, pulled out another dose and put it to Katrina's nostril. Again, she took a big whiff. Within moments, her mood changed. "Wow, that worked she said, you're right. I do feel better. Shit, I can dance all night!" They quickly left the restroom and continued to party until Rene decided to leave. It was around four in the morning. They exchanged numbers and left the club. Katrina drove to Chandra's place, which she now calls home. She was up waiting for her. Katrina let herself in with her key and went to the kitchen for a glass of water.

"Good morning," said Chandra.

"Good morning," Katrina replied. Chandra, looking her sister over, asked,

"Is everything okay?"

"Yes, everything's okay. I just decided to stop by the club to clear my head a little. I've been stuck in the house for weeks now feeling sorry for myself, so I decided to get out for a minute.

"Yes, the fresh air could do you some good; help to get your mind off things.

"Yeah, I was about to go crazy sitting in here crying all the time. The headaches are getting worse. I'm missing my children, and to top it all off, Tarik has taken all financial means from me. No cash, insurance, and no place to live. He's left me with nothing. He called me earlier to ask where he could send the divorce papers. I told him to mail them to Mom's house. I called Mom to let her know that he would be sending them. She immediately attacked me and asked me what I had done to Tarik. Of course, he told her the same lies that he's been telling her for years. She doesn't know what his family truly thinks about her. They've been providing for her all these years, and her head is so far up their asses that she can't see the truth.

Do you want to know what I did earlier today?"

"Tell me," Chandra said.

"I parked outside the kid's school and watched them play on the playground. Alexis was enjoying herself, but TJ looked sad, and he wasn't playing as much. It took all I had not to march into that school and take them right out of there. Tarik would have me arrested. I was forced to sign those papers years ago. I have no money and no place to live, and I can't work due to the headaches. How would I support us?"

"Katrina, you have the upper hand on him."

"How is that? I'll never find an attorney who'll fight his family and their team of attorneys. Even if I found an attorney who would be willing to take them on, what about the judge? They have every judge in this town on their payroll. Over the last several weeks, I've just about driven myself crazy trying to figure out what I could do to get my kids. I've come up with nothing."

"Well, I'm going to keep praying for you. You may not know what to do but our God does," said Chandra.

"No offense is, but I don't know what good that'll do. It hasn't seemed to work so far. But you keep on praying. Maybe He'll hear you, but He has never heard me. Why didn't He stop all the negative things from happening to me?" Chandra saw the frustration on her face and said, "Katrina, I can't tell you why you're going through this, but you can bet that it's not the end for you. God does love you and He will help you. You must believe that. You're too busy seeing the negative side of your situation. I know it's hard to see Him when you've been going through so much. Things will get better, so don't give up."

"Well, I'm glad somebody thinks so because I sure don't. I'm going to my room. I don't want to think about it right now. That's why I had to get out; so I could get it off my mind. I'm getting tired, and I need to get a little rest." Katrina went into her bedroom to lie down. She couldn't sleep, so she just lay there with her negative thoughts, staring at the ceiling. She could hear Chandra getting ready for work. After she left, Katrina went online to look for an attorney to help her with her divorce. She needed money, so she put her car up for sale, along with her wedding ring and other jewelry she wore when she was forced to leave home. She also wanted to get a little money to help Chandra with the bills. Tarik had recently purchased her a Mercedes SUV. She figured she could get at least ninety thousand dollars for it since it was worth at least half of that, and she'd hardly put any miles on it. Tarik paid fifteen thousand for the diamond earrings she was wearing. She also had a diamond necklace, bracelet, a watch, and all the gifts from her abusive husband after his many tirades. She had plenty more worth a fortune back at her home. She began thinking perhaps she should've hidden some for a rainy day. Tarik counted the money in the bank, but he never kept track of her jewelry. She could've made a small fortune in that alone, but she sold her belongings for a little over one hundred-ninety-thousand dollars. She put the money in her sister's bank account. She purchased a small used car for around eight thousand bucks. She paid off Chandra's home and bought a new bedroom, suit, and clothing for herself.

When their divorce was finalized, Katrina was left with nothing, but she was awarded joint custody of her children. Tarik never complied with the court order. All payments and gifts that Tarik used to send to Katrina's mother were immediately stopped, and she was unable to maintain the lifestyle that Tarik had set up for her. She had to rent her house out to make the last of the mortgage payments, so she moved in with Chandra and Katrina. She placed the blame on Katrina, citing that if she had been a better wife and mother, the divorce never would've happened. Katrina's mother was a constant thorn in her side with her continual criticisms and complaints. Katrina would stay away from their home to escape her nagging mother. She began a downward spiral into a constant state of depression and despair. Not only was she addicted to painkillers; she used cocaine regularly and was becoming a habitual user of the drug. She was hanging out more and more with Rene, who, as it turns out, was a call girl. Katrina and Rene went their separate ways after their brief friendship. Katrina's money had long since run out, and she began sleeping with men for money to support her habit. She was barely going around her family anymore and began walking the streets as a local prostitute, sleeping anywhere she could find. She tried staying high for as long as she could to escape the reality that she faced daily. Chandra was worried about her and constantly prayed for her while their mother continued to bad-mouth her.

While Chandra was on her way to work one morning, she saw her sister on the street looking ragged. Her hair was matted and mussed over her head, and her clothing looked worn. She immediately burst into tears. She pulled her car over and ran over to her sister. Katrina spotted her and tried to escape, but it was too late. Chandra had already taken her by the arm.

"Katrina!"

She took her sister and turned her towards her. She pulled her close and embraced her. Sobbing, she said, "I missed you, sis!" Chandra acted as if she didn't notice the dirt and filth on her sister. She just held her close and silently thanked God that she'd found her safe. Katrina was embarrassed and a little ashamed of her appearance. However, she was relieved to see Chandra. She lightly pushed her sister away and said,

"As you can see, I haven't been doing so well."

"Come on," Chandra said, walking her sister to her car. "I'm taking you home." Katrina had been in the streets for so long, and things were so bad that she willingly went with her. On the way home, Chandra asked, "Are you hungry?"

"Yes,"

"Well, let's stop and get you something to eat. What would you like?"

"It doesn't matter." Chandra got them both something to eat, and she drove them home. When Katrina entered the door, her mother was sitting on the sofa. Her mother said in disgust,

"Look at you! Is this what you've made of your life?"

"Mom, can we get in the door before you begin attacking her. Leave her alone. This is your daughter. You ought to be happy to see her."

"I'm sorry, but I lost my daughter long ago."

Katrina looked at Chandra and said, "I'm sorry sis, but this wasn't a good idea. I'll leave."

"Oh, no you will not," Chandra said as she walked towards her sister. This *is* your home. You helped to pay for this home. If it weren't for you, neither of us would be here. Now, Mom, you need to behave yourself. This is just as much Katrina's home as it is mine. If you'd like to leave, feel free to go. You have a home that you can go to, but my sister is not leaving."

"Oh, is this the way that you talk to your mother? Don't you have any respect for your elders? You're threatening to put me out?"

"Momma, nobody is threatening to put you out, but you need to respect my home. If you want respect, you must give it. Now I have allowed you to live here because you needed a place to stay to get your home paid off. Katrina gave fifty thousand dollars to pay this house off. You don't even pay bills here. I take care of you, and I let you live in a home that Katrina paid for.

Everything you have, you owe to Katrina." She walked her sister into her bedroom, and she ran her a hot bath. While Katrina was bathing, Chandra went back into the living room to talk with her mother. "Mom, I love you," she said. "I love my sister too. There's never going to be anything that you can say or do to get me to turn my back on her. For years, she's been trying to tell you what's been happening to her, and for years, you've turned a deaf ear to her."

"What has she been trying to tell me that I haven't been listening? She's a constant troublemaker. She had a good man and a good life. Now look at her, walking the streets like common trash. That man was good to her. That whole family was good to her. She messed all of that up for herself."

"No, what you mean is, you believe she messed it all up for you. Mom, I know you can't be that blind. Remember the black eyes and bruises, the busted lips, and overnight hospital stays. What did you think she was doing, hurting herself? Or did you just think she was accident-prone? That man was beating her. He and his family tormented her daily. She stayed because of her kids. You were the only selfish person reaping the benefits of her staying. You were blinded by all the money and gifts. But now you see how much they really care about you don't you?" Chandra shared every little detail of what Katrina told her to their mother. She didn't want to hear it, so she got her keys and began storming out.

"Where are you going, Mom?"

"I'm going to get some fresh air. For the past year, you've done nothing but make excuses for Katrina and you'll say anything about her ex-husband. If you would've stayed out of their business, perhaps they'd still be together. But no, you were too busy sitting around filling her head with all that nonsense about leaving. She constantly rebelled against him and her marriage. They told me everything. You'll never acknowledge that she's a total screw-up."

"Mom, I'm not going to argue with you. Do whatever it is you have to, but I want to make this clear to you. This is Katrina's home, and I don't want you doing or saying anything to make her feel uncomfortable. Do you understand me?"

Her mother grabbed her purse and put it in Chandra's face, and said, "You'd better put away all of your valuables." She walked out the door. Chandra took a deep breath and exhaled slowly. She went in to check on Katrina.

"Are you okay in here?"

"Yes, I feel much better after that hot bath."

"Well, you're home now. I don't ever want you to leave here again."

"What about Mom? I overheard you two talking. She still hates me, doesn't she?"

"Mom doesn't like anybody. She's just plain ornery. She's old and unhappy, and now that your marriage to that creep is over, she's broke and needs someone to blame."

"Mom has never had anything good to say to me all my life. I've never been able to please her. I know she hates me; she always has."

"Mom loves you, Katrina."

Unconvinced, Katrina looked at her sister and said, "Well if she does, she sure has a funny way of showing it. She hauled me off to live with Aunt Ellen and Uncle Ray. She never visited or called. She's never had anything good to say to me or about me. She calls herself a Christian, but she has so much hatred inside of her. I've never claimed to be a Christian. I've been good to people all my life. I've had to endure many hardships, and I still manage to treat people with dignity and respect. Mom doesn't know me, and she's never tried to get to know me. I've always wanted a relationship with her, but she's always pushed me away. She accepted Tarik as her son, but she rarely interacted with me. They would often talk on the phone for hours. I tried to tell her what was going on, but she decided that I wasn't telling the truth. Chandra, I've been on the streets for almost a year now, and I promise you, the things I faced in that home with that family were harsher than anything I've faced out there. I've made a mess of my life, and I know that. I hate being this way. I don't like my life, and I wish I could be a better person. I can't understand how I let my life turn out the way I have."

"Stop beating yourself up, Katrina," Chandra said, sitting next to her and holding her hand. Everybody makes mistakes. To tell you the truth, if I had to go through what you have, and I had to endure it alone, I probably would've lost it by now. I'm amazed you made it this far. I admire your strength, your love, and the sacrifices you made for the sake of your children and others. You're the most selfless person. God is going to bless you, watch what I tell you. He has something better in store for you than what you've been through. Trouble doesn't last always, and you will see God move on your behalf. Besides, He's never failed me."

"If God is so real then why have all of these bad things happened to me? Why are people like the McAllisters, so happy hurting everyone? They're some of the evilest people on the planet. They're worse than the mafia. If they can't pay you off, then they'll do everything in their power to try and destroy you. They prey on innocent people. They lie, steal, and cheat people out of everything. They have no morals, and they have violent tempers. I tell you on my last day there, I just knew I wouldn't make it out of there alive. And if Tarik had pulled the trigger that day; his mom was willing to cover it all up just like she has done all his life. Tarik used to love me, but his mother shut that down real quick. Trust me, if I had known I was going to go through all of that with him, I never would've had anything to do with him. He waited until after I had my children to show his ass. I haven't seen my babies in almost two years. I can't stand the pain so I try to drown out the physical and emotional pain with anything I can get my hands on. I want to tell you something. Before I saw you, I was at my breaking point, and I had decided I was going to end it all. I planned on taking my life. I was tired of battling the constant headaches and torment in my mind, that I'd chosen to die. I cried a little; I even tried to pray a little, hoping maybe your God would hear me. After not getting an answer, I made the final decision and that's when I saw you. Seeing you gave me a little hope, especially when you put your arms around me. I knew then perhaps somebody up there heard me. I love you Chandra. You're the only person in this world who loves me." Chandra held her sister and began crying.

"That's not true. TJ and Alexis, love you. God loves you, and so does Mom. She just doesn't know how to show it. I want you to know that I love you and I'll always be here for you. I don't care what you've done or what you will do. I love you unconditionally. I want to take care of you like you've taken care of others. I don't want you to leave here again. This is where you belong. Now I want you to get some rest, and we can talk about anything you want later. If you need anything, let me know. I'm here for you." Chandra left Katrina to her thoughts and went into the kitchen and fixed herself a cup of coffee. She went into her bedroom, got her bible, and began reading. She kneeled by her bedside to pray. *"Holy Father, I'd like to thank you for answering my prayers and bringing my sister home safely. I love you. I thank you for loving her and showing her your favor and for sparing her life. I pray that you show her your love* and kindness as you have shown me. I pray that you heal her of her headaches and the drug addiction. Let her know that you're with her and that she will be okay. I love you, and I thank you for answering my prayer. In Jesus' name." Chandra lay in her bed, sang spiritual songs, and continued to thank God for Katrina being home. She knew it was answered prayer that she happened to come along at the very moment that her sister had given up on life. While she was thinking, it had come to her mind that she had added Katrina onto to health insurance policy at her job six months earlier. She didn't know why at the time, but she had a strong urge to do so. Now it was becoming clear to her. Perhaps she could get some help for her drug addiction as well as for her headaches. She smiled and thanked God out loud. She settled in for bed. She heard their mother coming in the door. She went straight into her room and closed her door. She didn't come out for the rest of the night.

Chapter Five

Chandra got up early the next morning to fix breakfast for Katrina. She went into the kitchen where their mother was already there drinking a cup of coffee. "Good morning Mother." Her mom mumbled under her breath. "Good morning."

"Are you feeling any better today?"

"I'm doing well this morning. I see that your sister of yours is still in bed. Is she going to just lie there all day?"

"If she does, that'll be just fine with me. You need to show a little more compassion towards her. You don't know what she's been going through. Her body is tired, and not only that, but she is also emotionally drained. I'm going to let her take all the time she needs to heal and get better."

"I don't know what for; she ain't gonna do nothing but end up back on the streets. Once a drug addict, always a drug addict. She ain't gonna change," her mom said in a nasty tone.

"I believe in God's word, and His word says *the effectual fervent prayer of the righteous avails much,* and besides, she hasn't always been a drug addict. She's been through a lot; with all the abuse and then losing her children as she did, that's why she's on drugs."

Sipping from her coffee cup, her mom said, "I have been through a lot, too, but you don't see me out there using drugs, do you? Not everyone turns to drugs when they're having problems."

"Mom, not everyone reacts to emotional and physical trauma the same. You never know what the effects of hardship on a person could be. That girl has been through more hell than you or I put together. All you do is judge her, but it was by the grace of God you didn't have to endure the type of hardships she's had, and until you have walked a mile in her shoes, you have no authority to speak out against her negatively. God

114

will hold you responsible for what you say and do to her."

"So, it's my fault that she's on drugs and walking the streets. So, you say God's going to punish me when she's the one who's sinning."

"Mom, I think the greater sin here is your lack of love and your judgmental attitude toward God's child. You pride yourself on all your bible knowledge, and every time the church doors swing open, there you are on the front pew, but you don't live one bit of that word like you're supposed to. God is love. He loves all His children. The next time you're proudly carrying that Bible under your arm, why not open it and turn to the part about the prodigal son? And while you're at it, stop by the part about love. Oh, and I do believe there is something in there about judging not, lest ye be judged. There's more in there besides hell, fire, and damnation. Jesus said he came to save the sick and the lost. When was the last time you prayed for your daughter? When was the last time you sat down and talked with her without judging her? She used to come to you all the time, trying to share her feelings with you and what she was going through, but you turned your back on her and sided with her abusers. You've never believed in her. How many times have you even told her that you love her? You were all up in those in-laws of hers faces, throwing your daughter under the bus and accepting all their money, but you had nothing good to say about your daughter. Katrina has been nothing but good to us. When she was rich, she would send me and you all forms of financial assistance. Especially before they started limiting what she could give out. Don't you think it's odd that she left her home broke? Those people have millions of dollars, but your daughter left there without her children and any money. Katrina had every right to get custody of her children and half of their money. She was forced to leave, and her life was threatened. What would make a woman run from her own home and leave her children on her child's birthday? Now, I don't know what planet you've been living on, but you really need to open your eyes and stop being so blind to the things around you. Now, Mom, I'm not playing with you; if you bother my sister anymore, you're going to have to find somewhere else to live. I love you, but I love my sister too. I know that you still have a little blood-money saved up. You're not fooling anybody, and if you want to tell me that you don't, then you can always put that fancy home up for sale and buy yourself a small home somewhere. Now, I don't want any more trouble from you. At this point, my sister's well-being is in a critical state, and it's vitally important that she has someone on her side to help her heal during this difficult time in her life. If you can't be a part of her healing process, then you need to move on. I'm not going to allow you to hinder me from helping her. I can't make you love Katrina, but if you say one more negative word to her, I'll be forced to ask you to leave. Do I make myself clear mother?" Her mother looked at her with an evil eye. She didn't answer. "Mom! Do you hear me?"

"Yes, I hear you damn it! I don't know why you're talking to me like I'm a child; while you're quoting the bible, what happened to the part about honoring thy father and mother?"

"Mom, don't play with me about the word because I'm pretty sure it says something about parents not provoking their children. You need to read it and put it into practice. I love you, but you're not going to upset me and Katrina's home. We're more than willing to let you stay if you want, but you will not make us feel uncomfortable in our own home." Chandra went over to her mother and kissed her on the cheek. "I love you Mother." She walked over to the refrigerator, pulled the sausage and eggs, and started breakfast.

"How do you want your eggs cooked?"

"Scrambled, as usual," her mother said, picking up the newspaper and looking through it. "I want bacon instead of sausage." Chandra looked back at her mother and smiled. "I got you, Mom." Chandra fixed her mother's plate, got a tray, and placed Katrina's breakfast on it and her coffee. She went into her room. Chandra could hear Katrina in the bathroom. She placed the tray on the bed and went and knocked on the door. "Katrina, are you okay?" She could hear her vomiting. She began knocking on the door in a panic, "Katrina, are you okay?"

"Yes, I'm okay," Katrina yelled out. She came out of the bathroom. "Withdrawal's a bitch, and that greasy food I ate yesterday didn't help," she said, smiling at her sister.

"I made you breakfast. Do you have an appetite?"

"Well, my stomach's empty so I guess I need to eat. I just need some dry toast. How are you doing this morning?" Katrina asked.

"I'm more concerned about you at the moment."

"Oh, I'll be okay."

"Can I come in here and eat breakfast with you? I want to talk with you."

"Sure you can," Katrina said.

Chandra got her breakfast tray and went to Katrina's room, where they ate and talked. Katrina told Chandra about the horrors of living life on the streets. Katrina picked up a few tips for survival while she was out there. "When you found me yesterday, I had had a very bad week. I normally don't look as bad as I did, but I had gotten robbed that week by a guy posing as a john. I couldn't come up with my share of the loft money for that week. Business was very slow. I was hungry and feigning for a hit. My headaches were erupting like volcanos. I was missing my children, and I was very depressed. I looked horrible when you saw me. I was at my lowest point. When you came, you looked like an angel to me. I missed you so much, but I didn't want you to have to see me in the horrible state I was in. I wanted to visit you but with mom living here, I just couldn't take it. I would rather live on the streets than have to deal with her constant put-downs. Her words hit hard like a fist. I tell you, it's a different type of pain when your own mother doesn't give a damn about you. It seems like she takes pride in torturing me, like the McAllisters. She doesn't know how much I love her. I would do anything for her. I would even give my life for her if it meant that she could be happy."

Chandra said, "Well you don't have to worry about mom. She and I had a nice long chat, and she will not be bothering you anymore."

Katrina let out a laugh. "Yeah right, when have you ever known her to hold her peace about anything?"

"Trust me; you won't have any problems with her." Unconvinced Katrina said. "Okay if you say so." "I also wanted to talk with you about another subject," Chandra said. "During our open enrollment period, I added you to my health insurance plan. I want to get you in to see a doctor about your headaches. I want to make an appointment with your former doctor. Can we do that?"

"Oh Chandra, you didn't have to do that."

"Yes, I did. Girl it's the least I could do. First of all, if it wasn't for your connections, I never would've had that job in the first place. Thanks to you, I have a great job, a home that is paid for, and two or three extra dollars in the bank. You have come through for me so many times financially that I'm pretty well set up. We've been taking from you for years. It's time that we pay you back and take care of you for a change. Now, all I want you to do is rest and focus on getting better okay." Chandra looked at her sister and smiled. "Okay, sissy." Chandra took their trays and left the room. Thinking about her sister Katrina shook her head and smiled.

Chandra left for work. Katrina went to the kitchen to fix herself a cup of coffee. Her headache was back, and she didn't know how she was going to cope with the pain. Normally she would make a little money and score some coke to ease the pain. She grabbed her head, and she gritted her teeth. She was experiencing withdrawal symptoms. While she was standing at the counter, her mother walked into the kitchen. She saw Katrina holding her head moaning in pain.

"What's wrong with you?" she asked.

"Nothing, Mom," Katrina said through clenched teeth, trying to hold back the pain.

"I know what's wrong with you. You have been in that room getting high!"

"Mom, not right now."

"You need to get your life together. You may be fooling your sister but you're not fooling me one bit. She's always feeling sorry for you but look at you. You're high right now. Like I told her, you ain't gonna change.

"Mom, you don't know what you are talking about." Her mother went on and on continuing to verbally attack Katrina. She bolted out of the kitchen and went into her bedroom. She put her clothes on and left. With the unbearable pain in her head and the stress of her mother, she was forced to leave. She went back to the familiar. She needed some drugs and she needed them fast. She went to her old loft apartment to see if anybody there could help her score. Nobody came to the door. She left and began walking the streets looking for a customer. She noticed an old lady sitting at the bus stop on the corner. Although she was familiar with the stranger, they'd never actually spoken to one another. She was dressed in a neat floral dress, and her salt-and-pepper hair was pinned in a bun. She had a cute grandmotherly appearance, her face donning an infectious smile. Her hands rested on her purse as she patiently waited for her bus. Katrina was standing on the corner. This high-traffic area had been her usual hang-out where she saw many customers. She made lots of money there. She walked past the elderly lady who looked at Katrina and said, "Good morning baby."

"Good morning, ma'am," she said, walking past her again, looking down the road for a customer.

"May I speak with you for a minute?" The lady asked.

"Yeah, I guess so."

"Baby, I know you don't know me. My name is Effie. I come here almost every day to catch my bus and I see you out here often. I've noticed you hopping in and out of cars." Interrupting her, Katrina said,

"Look ma'am, I don't mean any disrespect, but I have to stop you right there. You don't know me like that. I don't need you all up in my business. I have a major headache, my mom has gotten on my last nerve, and I suppose you're here to preach to me too. Well, I don't want to hear it!" Frustrated with the world, Katrina was on edge, and she felt like she was about to snap. With a warm smile, the lady responded kindly.

"I apologize, but I'm not trying to interfere with your life. I just wanted to share something with you that the Lord wanted me to tell you. He wants you to know that He loves you and He's seen everything that's happened to you, all the pain and abuse towards you. He says that He's noticed all the beautiful things that you've done for His people. He wants to reward you for your kindness towards others. He's watching over you."

"Katrina was taken aback. "How could you know all of that?"

"The Lord revealed this to me."

"How could the Lord love me? Look at me! How could He possibly love a woman like me? I'm a drug addict and street woman."

"The Lord does love you. He sees your heart and it's a very beautiful heart. He doesn't judge your life by what you're doing now. Your actions don't define who you are.

You're in this difficult place for a reason. God is going to deliver you speedily and He will heal your body. He has also told me to tell you that there's a special prayer about two young children. He told me to tell you the answer is yes. He has heard your prayer, and He will do it for you!" Ms. Effie continued to tell Katrina more of her personal prayers and events of her life that only Katrina knew about. After the lady was done speaking, Katrina placed her hand over her mouth and said, "Oh my goodness, how could you have known all of that? Now I know that the Lord has sent you." The old lady reached into her purse and pulled out a small, green bible. She handed it to Katrina. Out of curiosity, Katrina asked, "What's this?"

"It's God's word. Whenever you're hurting or feeling lonely, If you're having feelings of despair, read this, and you'll feel better."

"Thank you, ma'am." Katrina stuffed the bible inside her purse. The bus came and the elderly lady got on it and left. Katrina was amazed at what she'd heard. She was still thinking about it when suddenly, she noticed a white Hummer with chrome rims stop at the light. The driver let his passenger window down to get a better view. Katrina, sizing him up to be a potential customer, began talking to the handsome guy. "What's up baby?" she asked.

Impressed with her striking beauty, firm ample breasts, tiny waist, and curvaceous frame, he said, "What's up with you baby? You're fine as hell!" After looking her over, he pulled over curbside and turned on his hazard blinkers. He exited his vehicle. He went over to Katrina. She glared at the six-and-a-half-foot, light-complexion man. His hair was light brown and wavy. His eyes were amber, with thick, bushy brows that appeared to be neatly trimmed. She thought, *"What kind of man trims his eyebrows?"* He was dressed as a businessman. She recognized the designer suit he was wearing. She was excited because she knew she'd hit the jackpot with this potential customer.

"Are you looking for a little fun this morning before you head off to that business meeting?"

"Nah baby, it ain't even that type of party. But I do have a way that you can make some real money.

You can stop hustling with this nickel-and-dime change. How much are you making anyway?"

"Now that's my business sweetie." Out of curiosity, she asked, "What do you mean you got a way that I can make some real money? How real are we talking?"

"About a few grand a night."

"Wow really? That's real money. Hey, wait a minute. I don't need a pimp; and by the way, what's in it for you? What's your cut?"

"I'm not a pimp. I'm a businessman. I create business opportunities for ladies like you. I'm a club owner. I own several different clubs in this town. I have some of the finest women working for me. I have a place where I know you will make some good money."

"Where is that?"

"The Honey Spot Club," he announced proudly while fixing his collar to his shirt.

"Oh, that's where all the wealthy men hang out huh? I heard about that place."

"Yeah, baby. that's my spot. You can make some good money there. I have nothing but high-profile clients there and they'll love you. You'll make plenty of money, and it'll get you off these streets, and you can make money in a safer environment."

"But I don't know anything about exotic dancing."

"I have a girl that I'm going to team you up with who will teach you everything. Don't worry, she won't put you out there if you're not ready. You can even work as a hostess while you train. Even they make thousands of dollars in tips nightly. Here's my card if you're interested and I do hope that you're interested."

"Oh, I'm very interested sugar. I'll be calling."

"Well, you do that. My name is Terrence, but they call me Tank. He reached into his pocket and pulled out a money clip. He counted out five, crisp, one-hundred-dollar bills and gave them to her. "Go and buy yourself something nice and get off of this corner," he said. He hopped back in his vehicle. "I'll be waiting for your call." He left and Katrina went and scored a little cocaine. She got her a hotel room. As she began to get high, her body didn't respond to the drugs as it normally did. She was in a euphoric state. She wasn't interested in getting high. The tight pressure in her head sent her into pain many times before it suddenly released, and immediately, her headache was gone. She was in awe. She placed what was left of the drugs back into the vial and she put it in a side pocket in her purse. As she was doing that, the bible that the elderly lady had given her fell out. She looked at it. Out of curiosity, she picked it up and opened it. She tried to read it, but she didn't understand what she was reading so she closed it. She looked up towards heaven and said, *"God, if you're really real, reveal yourself to me."* She opened the bible again and it fell open to Isaiah forty-one verse nine; *"I have called you. 'You are mine.' I* chose you and will not let you go. Don't be scared, I'm with you. I'm your God. I will help you. I will hold you with my right hand. Don't be afraid. I am here for you." Katrina read those verses over and over and as soon as she read them, she immediately understood them and was filled with joy. She reached for the phone to call Chandra. When she answered, she told her everything that had happened. Chandra was happy for her sister. She was happy that God was finally revealing Himself to her. She knew that God was answering her prayers. Katrina ended the call with her sister. She gathered her things and went home. Her mother had already left. She was relieved because she didn't feel like having another run-in with her. Katrina placed her things in her room. She heard the doorbell ring and ran to answer it. It was the mail carrier. He had a certified letter for her. She signed for it and opened it. It was from Tarik's attorney. It was a letter informing her that Tarik was petitioning the court, requesting that her parental rights be terminated permanently. She was crushed. She fell to the floor and started crying uncontrollably. Katrina got up and went into her bedroom. She spread the contents of the letter over the bed. She got on her knees and she began to pray for the first time in her life. Katrina prayed from her heart with urgency, feeling that this was the last chance to get her prayers answered. *"God, I know that I'm the last person that you want to hear from right now, but I need to talk to you. I know that I have made a mess of my life. I want to be better, but I need your help. I can't do it alone. I have tried over and over to quit doing drugs, but I just can't seem to stop. Today was the only good day that I've had in a while. If you'll help me to get off drugs and give me back my children, I promise I'll serve you and I'll raise my children to serve you. Please don't let Tarik terminate my parental rights. My children are all I have in this world besides my sister."* She continued praying and crying. After a while, she got off her knees and lay down on the bed. She was afraid. She picked up her bible and opened it. The first scripture that she came to was Isaiah forty-three and verses five and six. It read of promises of gathering her and her children together. *She* closed it and thought to herself that it was merely a coincidence. She opened it again, this time to Isaiah in chapter sixty, verse four. It read of the promise of bringing her children home. She couldn't help but laugh. She thought it was amazing how God had gotten her to laugh when she was in such a panic. She smiled and prayed again. She thanked God for hearing her. She marked the scriptures in her bible. She started thinking of ways to get money for an attorney. She knew she was going to need a good one, and she was now willing to fight Tarik. She needed to make a lot of money, but she didn't know how she was going to get it. She thought about the guy that she had met earlier. She took the card out of her purse and called the number on the card. She told the young lady who answered the phone who she was. "Honey Spot, how may I help you?"

"Umm, hi. My name is Katrina. Mr. Terrence gave me a card. He told me to call."

"Yes, Katrina. Terrence told me you'd be calling. We've been waiting for you." Katrina made an appointment to go that evening. She drove to the store and bought a few items with the money that Terrence had given her earlier. Instead of going home, she went to her hotel room, dressed, and left for the club. Before she could make it inside the club, patrons were coming on to her and giving her their business cards. She took the cards and proceeded to enter the swanky two-story building. She looked around, and she could tell this was no low-class strip joint. It was pure money, all set in a luxurious atmosphere. She noticed a large marble statue of a beautiful female in a seductive pose, set inside a large, multicolored water fountain. Beautiful wall art of lovely women tastefully donned the walls. Angel, the young lady that she had spoken with on the phone, greeted her. She was very pretty. She was around five feet nine inches, and she was wearing a white fishnet mini skirt with white lace and diamond studded see-through bra. She was also wearing a diamond choker around her neck and diamond earrings. The shoes that she was wearing were diamond-studded five-inch heels.

"Hello, I'm Katrina," she said, introducing herself.

"I'm Angel. Come with me." While heading towards the office, Katrina noticed beautiful young women dancing on the first and second floors. They had tight, toned bodies. She began to feel a little intimidated when she noticed their beauty. She thought, *"What in the hell am I doing here? I'm too damn old for this. And look at their bodies. They look amazing, looks as if they just stepped out of a swimsuit magazine."* Patrons sat at the bar eating their meals while others sat in private sections enjoying their female companions.

She was escorted into Angel's office. "Have a seat," she said. Katrina was seated in the chair adjacent to the desk, and Angel took her seat behind the desk.

"I will need a copy of your driver's license and social security number. You will get paid each night once we tally up. Our clients don't tip dancers on the floor. They purchase a temporary card assigned to them by the club with each girl's information. They pay the cashier before they check out for each girl who worked for them. That money is assigned to your account. If you owe the club, that fee will be taken from your pay, and you will be paid the rest in cash. You can choose to become an employee of the club, and we'll handle all the IRS and other employment insurance. Alternatively, you could be your own boss by remaining independent, leaving you to handle your own legal paperwork. Either way, we will report accurately what we pay to the authorities. Tank runs a legitimate business. Here's a pamphlet explaining everything."

Katrina took the pamphlet and briefly looked it over. Angel then asked,

"How tall are you?"

"I'm around five-five."

"How old are you?"

Before Katrina could answer, Angel said, "You look about twenty-five or twenty-six years old." Katrina laughed out loud.

"I'll take that," she said, handing Angel her driver's license.

"You look great. What size do you wear? You look like a size two."

"I am," she said.

Katrina had lost some weight due to her drug use. Angel talked with Katrina a bit more, giving her a brief rundown of the rules and regulations of the club. To protect the club, she copied her driver's license for their records to prove that she was of legal age. After completing the necessary paperwork, she walked Katrina to another room resembling a small boutique. It was filled with all sorts of exotic clothing. Anything you could think of, they had it. There were shoes in every style and size, leather camisoles, spiked clothing, and many other styles of sexy costumes. A young lady inside was stocking the place and arranging costumes for display.

"That's Candy over there. If you need anything, she'll assist you. You must pay for these items. For your convenience, you'll be offered a line of credit, or you can pay for it with your tips. You can always bring your own costumes, but if you forget or want something different, we have it all right here. We have a hairstylist and make-up artist on site. As long as the club is open, someone is always here to assist you. We're open every day but Sunday. For some reason, Terrence won't do business on Sundays. He tells us all that we need to have our asses in church on Sunday. Strange behavior for a man in this business, but he's the boss." They continued to tour the club. She introduced Katrina to everyone that she would need to meet to get prepared for a show.

"Will you be starting tonight?" Angel asked.

"Yes, I guess I will."

"Will you be dancing, or would you like to wait tables first?"

"I think I will wait tables tonight." She said unsure of herself.

Okay, but you still need to dress up to do that. She took Katrina to the stylist. They got her hair and make-up done, she picked out an outfit and shoes and she got dressed and was sent back to Angel. Katrina looked at her hair and make-up. She looked as if she'd just stepped out of a magazine. She was amazed at how different she looked. She walked into where Angel was standing. "Girl, look at you! You don't even look like the person who walked in here a while ago. Shit, you're hot! You're going to make loads of money." She took Katrina to the bar and handed her over to the bartender. Katrina caught on fast. She waited tables all night, making tons of tips, and she received plenty of requests. Many wealthy men were there, and each one of them begged her for a dance or gave her their cards, wanting to see more of her. She couldn't believe the attention she was receiving. They weren't asking for sex but simply a dance, and they were willing to pay huge sums of money. "Damn, all this time I've been having sex for a few bucks here and there and these guys are willing to pay me just to dance. Terrence was right about this. Katrina was excited and happy to be working at the club. That night alone, she made almost two thousand dollars in tips from just waiting tables. She could hardly believe it. She allowed Angel to teach her dancing techniques and began dancing on her second night. That night, she made close to six thousand dollars. She was inundated with requests to do private shows. On her first week alone, she made more than twenty-eight thousand dollars. She went back to her room that evening and counted her money. She had been staying at a hotel because she didn't want to come in and out of Chandra's place late every evening. It was late Saturday night. As she lay across her bed and read her bible, she considered attending church the next day with her sister.

Chapter Six

Chandra was happy that Katrina attended church with them. After the service, they went for lunch, along with their mother. Their mother hardly said two words to either of them. They didn't mind; they ignored her silent treatment and enjoyed their dinner while chatting as if she wasn't there. They were used to her negative behavior, and they were not about to let her spoil their afternoon. After lunch, they dropped their mother off at home, and they went to catch a movie. Afterwards, they went out for coffee and talked. Katrina told Chandra all about the club and the money she was making. Chandra didn't like it, but she never attacked her sister for anything she did. Besides, she showed no signs of drug use, and she was looking a lot better. To top it all off, she went to church with her that day. Chandra realized that recovering from drug use was a work in progress. She noticed the positive changes in her sister. She also noticed that she hadn't complained of headaches all day. She was curious, so she asked,

"How have those headaches been lately?"

"A funny thing happened last week; I went to my room, and I tried to get high, but I couldn't. I felt something snap inside my head, but in a good way. I felt good, but I wasn't high. I haven't had one headache since that day, nor have I had any drugs or desired any. I don't know why, but I feel that I'm healed. I think your prayers are working for me."

"God is good," Chandra said.

"Yes, He is!" Katrina said.

They enjoyed their evening and went home.

After playing a game of checkers, they went to bed. Katrina wanted to surprise Chandra with breakfast the following morning, so she woke up early and prepared breakfast. She cooked for the entire household. She made French toast, bacon and eggs, sausage links, grits, and coffee. The smell permeated the home. It awakened her mother. She showered and went into the kitchen, thinking that Chandra had made breakfast. When she saw Katrina in the kitchen, she produced a sour expression towards her.

"Good morning, Mom," Katrina said, smiling at her. Would you like me to fix you a plate?"

"No, I'm not hungry all of a sudden."

She poured herself a cup of coffee instead and took a seat at the kitchen table. Chandra walked into the kitchen, fully dressed.

"Something sure smells good this morning," she said.

"Doesn't it, though?" Katrina asked.

"Mom's not hungry today, so you and I will have to eat all of this, or it'll go to waste."

"Are you kidding? Mom doesn't want any of these hot, buttery French toasts or these steaming hot, buttery grits. Girl, is that cheese in those grits?"

"You know it, Havarti, and they are hella good." Chandra looked at her mother and said, "Mom, you don't know what you're missing." She was staring at the food. She took a sip of her coffee, swallowing hard, trying to get it to fill her up. "I'm okay," she said while eyeing the delicious food.

The girls began eating breakfast. Their mother couldn't take it any longer. She fixed herself a plate and began eating. Chandra and Katrina looked at her and smiled. "What are y'all looking at? Pour me some more coffee!" she said in a snappy tone. Chandra did as she was told and said to her mother, "I think it's time that you two had a long talk."

"I do too. Whenever you're ready, Mom, I am."

"Can't I enjoy a good breakfast without you two hussies bothering me?"

Chandra finished her breakfast and got up from the table. She said her goodbyes and went to work. Katrina finished her breakfast and cleaned the kitchen. She got her Bible, sat on the sofa, and began reading it. Her mother walked in and saw her and said, "You need to get your life together first before you start reading that bible. Once you get your life right, then God will hear you, so put down that Holy word before lightning strikes you."

"Mom, why are you always on me like this? What do you think I'm doing? I'm trying to get my life together."

"Maybe if you would do right, I wouldn't have to be on you all the time. Besides, somebody needs to talk to you. I'm not like your sister. I'm not going to babysit you while you're in the middle of your mess. I'm going to stay on you until you get it right."

"I don't need your kind of help, Mom. I may not be a holy roller like you but I'm learning that God loves me regardless of who I am and what I've done. You've been a Christian all your life and you don't seem to know that God loves us all. The Lord is working with me right now and if you would leave me alone and allow Him to work, then everything will work out fine. I love you, Mom, I honor you, and I respect you, but I answer to God, and I don't feel that He's condemning me, and I'm pretty sure that He's not pleased with the way you've been treating me. All you had to do was pray for me and believe in me, but you chose to treat me harshly, and you've had a negative attitude towards me since I could remember. This didn't just start with the drug use. Now what I want to know is, why you seem to hate me so much. You even sided with my ex-husband and his family over me even though he was abusing me, and his parents continued to hold my life hostage. I want to tell you something, Mom, and this time, I want you to hear me out and hear me good. Now you know that I don't have any reason to tell you any lies. I'm going to tell you everything in detail and I'm begging you to listen. You don't have to believe me, but you do need to hear this. Katrina told her mother everything. She told her the complete horrors of her ordeal with the McAllister family. She told her about the abuses, about the threats, and how they threatened the lives of her family. When she was done, her mother sat there with her mouth hanging open. Her mother shed a tear, and instantly, she realized how misguided she was about everything.

"Mom, are you okay?"

Her mother looked at her and said, "I'm so sorry Katrina. I don't know what to say." She left Katrina sitting on the sofa. She was emotional about what she was hearing, as if she was hearing it for the first time. She went into her bedroom and cried for a better part of an hour. While there, she prayed and asked the Lord to forgive her for the way she had treated Katrina over the years, and she prayed for her. She had a change of heart, and she knew that she needed to fix things between her and Katrina. She went into her closet and pulled out a small black safe. She took out a large envelope with pictures and letters in it. Also, inside was a small lock of hair with a pink ribbon wrapped around it. She went into the living room where Katrina was still sitting reading her bible. She sat next to her. "I have some things I want you to see."

"What is it, Mom?" She looked in her mother's hands and noticed a few black-and-white photographs of a young couple.

"These are letters from your father to me while we were dating. They were pictures of us when we were young."

"My father?"

"I was seventeen when I met your father. It was on a Sunday after church. My daddy allowed me to go with my friends to the local ice cream shop. Your father was there with his friends. He came over to me and he laid on the charm. He purchased my ice cream, and he asked me if I wanted to ride with him. He was twenty-six years old. He had his own place, and he owned a very nice pickup truck. He was so handsome. All the girls liked him, but he wanted me. I thought I was so lucky that this much older, perfect guy wanted to be with me. I told him that he would have to ask my father's permission if he wanted to date me. He smoothed-talked his way out of asking for my father's approval. I was so infatuated with him that I found myself sneaking out to meet him. I was lying to my parents, telling them that I was with my friends. He would take me down by the creek and we would talk and talk. He got me to trust him. I was so in love with him. We would sit out under the stars and plan our life together. He would tell me stories of how he would marry me and take me away from that little country town to live in a big city. He said anywhere I wanted to go; he would take me. One night he brought some wine and a blanket. I drank it with him, and we made love right there in that field. I was hooked on him. Every night I would sneak away from my home and meet him in that field. We would drink wine and make love. When I found out I was pregnant, I was so excited to tell him. I was afraid of what my parents would say, but I knew that he was going to take care of me, so I told him. He went crazy. He began insulting me and telling me that you were not his child. I was devastated by his reaction. I went home and confessed to my parents. I told them everything. Daddy went to talk to him. Well, come to find out he was already married, and he had two children. Daddy took his shotgun down there and threatened to kill him. He ran like a coward. He moved and I haven't heard from him since. He's never seen you, nor has he come back to inquire about you. These are the only photos that we took together when we all used to hang out together before we started seeing each other. After he left town, my young mind was confused. Rumors were circulating and I felt like an outcast. While I was pregnant with you, I drank heavily. After giving birth, my parents sent you to your aunt and uncle who took care of you until I could get better. I continued drinking for a couple of years and I ran the streets something awful. I was in bars at all times of the day and night. Finally, I came out of the streets and started going to church. I got my life together, and that's when I met Chandra's father. We married and stayed together until he died. I tried to forget my past and it seems that you were always a painful reminder of that past I wanted so much to forget. These letters are the ones your father used to send me before we split. To this day, I have no idea of why I've kept them." She handed Katrina the letters. "I want to ask you to forgive me. I have been blaming you for my inner demons. When you became addicted to drugs, that's when it all came back to my mind. I was forced to remember, and it seems the more I attacked you, the more I could hide behind my own mistakes. I mistreated you. I apologize to you." As soon as her mother apologized, healing began to take place in her heart. Her mother began to cry. Katrina placed her arms around her mother, and they both fell to their knees to pray. Later, they talked for what seemed to be hours. Katrina's mom filled in all the gaps in her life, telling her everything. They spent the rest of the afternoon together. Afterwards, Katrina went online to look for an attorney for her upcoming court day. One ad, in particular, caught her eye. It was Sloane & Associates. Their ad mentioned that he never lost a case. She called and made an appointment for the following day. She wanted to go to the club that evening so that she could make a little more money to go along with what she already had for her attorney. She went to the mall to buy herself some things to wear to the club then drove on over to the Honey Spot Club. It was still kind of early, so she went into the dressing room, sat down, and read a little bit of her bible.

Some of the other dancers began showing up. When she heard them coming in, she hurriedly put her bible underneath her bags. She spoke to the girls, and they all chatted for a while. They didn't look like they were going to leave anytime soon, so she gathered her things and went to the shower. As she was showering, she said a brief prayer.

She went to the make-up room to get her make-up done. While doing that, images of her children flashed through her head. She secretly started praying for them again. She left the make-up area and went to get her hair styled. She felt the urge to leave the club. Katrina was having a change of heart, and she wanted to leave but talked herself out of it. She got dressed and it was time to go on the stage. Her music began but she didn't seem to hear it. Angel motioned for her to go on stage. She went out and began her performance. She looked over at the audience intently. Onlookers were enjoying her show, but Angel could tell something was off about her. She thought Katrina was nervous. As Katrina looked into the audience, she was shocked to see her children standing there among the patrons. In a panic, she turned to leave the stage. As she was making her exit, she looked again and realized it was only a figment of her imagination. She shook it off, went back, and finished the show. She suddenly heard a voice. It wasn't an audible voice, but she could almost hear it with her ears and at the same time within her heart and mind. It was a still, small voice that said, *"Katrina, I want you to quit dancing."* She continued to dance but at a slower pace. Customers were trying to tip her, but she lost her focus as the voice continued. *"It's time for you to leave this place. I want you to quit dancing."* She heard herself say aloud, "Yes Lord." She finished her show, got dressed, and went into her dressing room.

Angel followed her. "Katrina, are you okay?"

"Yes, I'm okay, why do you ask?"

"Well, it seemed like something was wrong with you out there on the stage."

"I'm good; I'm just a little tired. Katrina got her things and left the club. She went home and prayed.

Meeting with the Attorney

It was Tuesday morning and Katrina pulled up to Sloane & Associates Law firm for her appointment. She was impressed by the building. It was an eighteen-story office building with many offices. The Sloane name was carved into the building. The landscape was beautiful. Katrina began wondering if she could afford to hire them. She didn't think about it long. She went inside with confidence. When she made it inside, there was a kind young lady at the front desk who greeted her with a smile.

"Welcome to Sloane & Associates, how may I help you?"

"Hi there, I'm here to see Mr. Harold Sloane. My name is Katrina McAllister."

The young lady handed her a form and said, "Fill this out for me. I'll have you in to see Mr. Sloane as soon as you're done."

Katrina took a seat in the luxurious posh office. After she was done with her form, she took it to the receptionist. The receptionist informed Mr. Sloane that she was ready. She pointed Katrina towards Mr. Sloane's office. On her way back, she noticed a tall, handsome, black man approaching her. His deep brown skin caught her eye. He was wearing a navy-blue Armani suit and tie with a perfectly polished pair of Berluti Scritto leather shoes. She fixed her eyes on him and began walking toward him. She walked up to him and introduced herself.

"Hi there, I'm Katrina McAllister," she said giving him her hand for a handshake.

"I'm Harold Sloane," he said shaking her hand.

"We spoke on the phone the other day."

"Oh no," he said. "You're looking for my father. I'm Harold Sloane Jr., his son."

"Oh, I'm sorry," Katrina said laughing nervously.

"So, you're not an attorney?"

"Goodness no. That's my father's field. I handle all the finances for all our companies. Have you ever heard of a little company called Harolco Corporation?"

"Of course, I have. Who hasn't heard of them? I heard they did millions in business last quarter alone. Good move on deciding to go global."

"Well, that's our company."

"Okay, now It's all coming together. Yes, I remember seeing you many times in publications and on the news. I hardly recognized you. You're a brilliant businessman. You guys have turned what was a small family business into an empire. Not to mention all the real estate and commercial properties you guys own. Why you guys own half of this state as well as surrounding areas. You guys have your hands in everything."

"Yes, we're not the ones to turn down lucrative opportunities and we love investing in our communities and building them back up. I still personally oversee the entire operation. But I don't want to talk about that. What I would like to know is, how may I see you again?" Harold stood there staring into her eyes. Still holding her hand, he said. "I'm sorry to stare but you're beautiful."

"Thank you," she said with a shy smile.

"So, are you going to give me an answer?"

Katrina was excited about the prospect but then she thought about her past and said, "Right now is not a good time for me. I have some things in my life that I need to work out first. I don't need to bring anybody into my madness."

"Nonsense; how about we go and share small talk over a cup of coffee?"

"I wish I could. I'm in a very bad place in my life right now and..."

"And you need to get all of that off your mind and have a cup of coffee with me. I'm not asking for a commitment, only a little bit of your time. What do you say? Will you?" Katrina exhaled. She could see the gentleman wasn't going to take no for an answer.

"I guess I can. It's only coffee. Yes, I'll go." They exchanged information and said their goodbyes. Katrina went in to see the attorney. He met her at the door. He looked to be sixty-five years old. He was around five-eight in height, with a light complexion and a greying hairline. He looked very friendly. He introduced himself to her and showed her to her seat. As she was sitting, he walked to his desk and took his seat. On his desk, she noticed a bible and a picture of him and his wife. She smiled thinking it was a good sign so far.

"How are you, Ms. McAllister?"

"I'm doing well."

"How may I help you today?" They shared small talk, and she began to tell him her issue. "I haven't seen my children in almost two years. My ex-husband has refused to allow me to see them. As a condition of our divorce decree, I'm allowed non-supervised visits and he's chosen to ignore our court order." She handed him her divorce decree and also the termination documents. She then told him of the horrible abuses that she suffered at his hands. She continued with her story.

"I mean, the abuse was so severe that visiting the hospital was a normal routine. As a result of the last beating, I was in a coma, and I was hospitalized for several months. I'd been suffering ongoing effects like severe headaches and body aches. Some days I just hurt all over. It was only here recently that I've been able to get through the day without any pain. I have to admit that I went into a state of depression and I kind of checked out of life for a year or so. I hit rock bottom with no one to turn to. The police wouldn't investigate the abuse. Each time I went to them they would send for

Tarik, and he would come to the police station and pick me up. Any outside help I tried to receive, or if I tried leaving, he would sabotage it. After a severe beating, he locked me in one of our rooms for several days with no food or water and forced me against my will to sign a contract stating that if we ever divorced that I would not seek custody of our children. When he finally let me out the chief of police was sitting downstairs in our dining room. At that point, I didn't know if he knew what had happened to me and refused to help. Needless to say, I felt hopeless. Knowing the power that my former in-laws held in this town and knowing I wouldn't receive help, I found it would be better if I stayed for the sake of my children. Tarik doesn't love our children. He only has them to keep me from getting their money. The thing is, I have no desire for their money. At his request, I quit college to care for our son. Thinking that I would be able to go back after they were older, I did as he requested. I wasn't allowed to finish my education. He would make every excuse for me not to. He was afraid that I would become independent of him. I'm really afraid for my children. Although he's never physically harmed them, he has been verbally aggressive with our son. I'm afraid that he will begin to get violent with him if he hasn't already. He has no control over his temper. I want my children out of that environment. Nobody there truly has their best interest at heart."

When she finished telling him her entire story, she told him who the family was. My ex-husband is Tarik McAllister. His parents are Frances and Frank McAllister. She was sure that after hearing the McAllister's name he would turn her away and refuse to accept the case, but much to her surprise he was not at all intimidated by them.

"Ms. McAllister, I'm so sorry to hear about all the pain and trauma you've been through. My heart goes out to you. I can see that our system has failed you, but rest assured, I will not allow that to happen again. Not everyone in this town is on their payroll. Actually, there are many good people out there who have not allowed their money to dictate their actions. I have never been fond of the family. Don't worry about a thing. I'll take care of everything." Katrina had complete confidence in him. She could tell that she was going to like him. "The first thing I'm going to do is to get your case back in court, and I'll file for a motion of enforcement. I'll also work to help you get full custody of your children and any monies that you have coming to you regarding this case."

"I'm not asking for any of their money; I only want my children."

"With all due respect, Ms. McAllister, giving all you've been through, that family owes you, and I'm going to see to it that they pay." Katrina was very pleased with her meeting with her new attorney. After their consultation, he asked Katrina for permission to pray with her. To her, that was unusual for an attorney. She gladly accepted. After he was done praying, she gave him her cheek. They talked a bit more and she left. She was feeling optimistic. On her way home, she called Chandra to let her know what happened. After hearing everything Katrina had to say, Chandra said, "See, I told you everything was going to work out for you. That's our Heavenly Father answering our prayers. He's not finished either. Watch what He does next! He is truly awesome."

"Girl, I had given up on the God thing. It seemed utterly futile to pray. Each time you told me that you were praying for me, I used to say to myself, *I don't know what, for it never works,*" but He has been showing me things here and there, and I'm starting to believe in Him."

"Well, when you begin to develop a relationship with Him, you'll love Him even more. It takes time, but you'll begin to trust Him more and more, and then you'll realize that He's been there all along. Everything you've been through was designed so that you'll be a testimony to others who will need to hear what you have to say. When I went to Father to pray for you, He assured me that He was in control, and He was going to deliver you from all you were going through. It hurt me to watch what was happening knowing you didn't understand, but I've always remained confident that He was a God of His Word and He was going to do exactly what He promised!"

"Sis, I tell you what, I admire your faith because I've never had any." Katrina laughed.

"I love you," she said to Chandra.

"What time will you be home?" Chandra asked.

"I'm on my way there now."

"Well, I know that you don't want to have to eat dinner with Mom, so how about we go out to dinner this evening?"

"Oh, I forgot to tell you, Mom and I had a nice long talk. I don't think we'll have as much turmoil in the house anymore."

"Girl, please tell me you didn't curse the old lady out! Wait a minute; you didn't kill her, did you?"

"No, she's still alive. She's too damn stubborn to die." They laughed. Katrina told Chandra everything.

"God is good!" Chandra said after hearing all that happened with her sister and mother. Why don't we all just go out to dinner tonight?"

"Well sis, I have accepted an invitation to coffee this evening."

"Oh yeah, with whom may I ask?"

"I'm going with Harold Sloane's son.

Oh really, you mean to tell me that the richest bachelor in this state wants to have coffee with my sister."

"Yes, it seems as if he does."

"Well, if you accepted, then he is one lucky guy!"

"Aww sis, you're so sweet!" Katrina said. I'm heading home now to get ready for that. I'll see you when I get there." They ended their call.

Katrina made it home. After picking out something to wear for her coffee date she went to fix herself a snack. Her cell phone rang. It was Harold Sloane Jr.

"Hello, Katrina. How are you doing this evening?"

"Hello Harold, I'm doing well, and you?"

"I'm great. I was just calling to confirm that you were still going to join me tonight for coffee."

"Yes, I'll be able to join you." Harold gave her the address of where to meet him. She arrived at the coffee shop. She noticed Harold sitting in a black SUV. The evening lights shone on his deep brown skin. She noticed a smile on his face as she appeared in his view. He hopped out of his vehicle and began walking towards her vehicle. He helped her out of her car. He wasn't wearing a suit, but he was dressed stylishly in a nice shirt and dressy slacks. He took Katrina's hand, and she caught a whiff of his cologne. *"He looks amazing. Oh, he smells so good,"* she thought. She smiled as he led her inside and to her seat. He pulled the chair out for her and gently pushed it in as she took her seat. He complimented her on her beauty, and he took his seat.

"I'm so glad you decided to join me tonight. You were so hard on me that I didn't think I stood a chance."

"I thank you for inviting me," she said while looking at him curious as to what he was thinking. She was glad to be there. She wasn't expecting much to come of the friendship. She felt it best if Harold knew the truth about her so he would not continue and try to court her. So, she decided she would be forthcoming about her life. Although she was impressed by him, somewhere deep inside, she felt that she didn't deserve a man like this especially given all the dirty things she had done in the streets. She didn't tell him about her past right away. She allowed the conversation to play itself out. They were having a great time, and he was enjoying her company. When it seemed as if Harold was about to get a little too close to be suggesting more than a friendship, she decided to tell him everything. "Harold", she said, "I need to tell you about me." She put her coffee down and said, "I don't think that we should see each other beyond tonight. I want you to understand that it's just not a good time for me to be dating right now."

He looked at her and said, "You tried to tell me that earlier. So, tell me what are these troubles that you say are keeping such a lovely lady like you from dating?"

"You don't know what's really going on."

"From what I can see, you have a beautiful spirit."

"I'm glad you think so. You're just looking at things on the surface. You really don't know what's going on with me. Since I won't be seeing you after tonight, I'm going to tell you everything." She did. Katrina told him about her marriage and the abuse, to the street life and the strip club. She didn't put any cut on it. She told him everything just the way it happened.

He looked at her and said, "Now that wasn't so hard, was it? I can see that you've been through a lot. All you need is someone to love you through the pain. From what you say, your sister has been a constant support throughout your ordeal."

"So, you understand why we can't see each other after tonight?"

"I'm glad you told me the truth about you Katrina. Most women would've hidden something like that from a guy. Especially a guy like me because they feel that they would be blowing an opportunity at what they perceive would be a good life. The reason I'm single and I've never married is because a lot of women I've met know me and my family status. They feel that being in a relationship with me would boost their financial status. In the beginning, they're sweet and innocent but their true motive comes through in the end. When I saw you, I knew there was something special about you. Your willingness to throw away your chances of dating a wealthy person to protect me from your past is a wonderful gesture. What you've told me here tonight has not deterred me from wanting to get to know you. I would love to be a friend and another form of support for you. I like you. I believe you're a good woman and it sounds as if you're a great mother. You got side-tracked by a little adversity. You need a friend. Why not allow me to walk this journey with you?"

"Why would you do something like that for me?"

"Look, when I first saw you, I could tell that you were somebody special. You're so beautiful. Besides, I felt something in my spirit about you. When I shook your hand, I felt the anointing of God on you. Something inside me said she's the one. I know the voice of God when I hear it and each time I follow His leading, I've always succeeded in life. I knew that our meeting was not by chance but by divine appointment. The more I talk with you, the more I want to get to know you. I'm even dreading for this night to end because that means I have to say goodbye to you.

"You're so sweet, you're just being kind," she said.

"I'm just being honest. As I said, nothing you've shared here with me tonight has deterred me from wanting to get to know you better. The only person who can stop this friendship from going any further is you. Now, I wish you would relax and realize that you've found a friend who will care for you no matter what. It's a new chapter in your life so can we forget about your past for a while and enjoy our evening?"

"Well, if you're still willing to be my friend after I've shared all the sordid details of my life with you, then I suppose I can put it all behind me." She smiled and put her coffee cup to her lips and drank. They talked for a few more minutes.

"It's a nice evening out; would you like to go for a walk?"

"I don't mind," she said. They left the coffee shop and went for a brief walk. They continued to get to know each other. Harold was a great guy, he was thoughtful, funny, and full of charm and he adored Katrina. He saw no signs of a woman who had suffered at the hands of life's turmoil. Katrina found that she was enjoying herself. Harold made her laugh and his outlook on life amazed her. He had all the charm of a man's man, but he was playful fun, and funny. They were having such a good time together that they lost track of time. They noticed that all the shops on the row were turning their lights out and closing for the evening. That's when they noticed the time.

"I'd better get you back to your car before it gets too late," he said. They headed back to their vehicles. As they walked up to her vehicle, Harold began to drag his feet to prolong the last few minutes of their night. "I enjoyed your company tonight Katrina. I thank you for accepting my invitation."

"I enjoyed myself as well." She walked up to her car and pressed the alarm. Harold opened her door for her. As she got ready to get in the car, he asked for permission to hug her. She said yes. He felt that asking for a kiss would be a bit much and he didn't want to scare her off. As he hugged her gently, she inhaled. His arms felt great wrapped around her. She had to loosen her embrace. She was getting lost in the moment. They said their goodbyes and she drove away leaving him standing there with a smile on his face. Before she could make it to the next street, her phone was ringing. She answered and heard; "Dinner tomorrow night?"

She smiled to herself and said, "I'll let you know tomorrow."

"I will be looking forward to your call."

"Okay goodbye," she said.

Before he ended the call, he said. "I really would like to see you again Katrina."

"You will."

"I sure hope so." They ended their call. Katrina smiled. She began wondering, *"was it really real? Could he truly be interested in her?"* She didn't see how, given what she told him about her life. She thought he seemed sincere and not at all bothered by her past. Perhaps he really was interested. She shrugged her shoulders and turned the volume up on her radio to drown out her thoughts. "We'll see," she said out loud. She drove home where Chandra was up waiting on her. She put her things on the sofa and plopped down and exhaled with a smile on her face.

"Tell me all about it girl!" Chandra said.

Chapter Seven

Katrina's attorney had gotten her case back before a judge. This one was far more reputable than the one her ex had used. As they were sitting outside the courtroom, she noticed Tarik and Sharice walking toward the courtroom. Her heart began to race. She didn't want any conflict with him but knowing Tarik, he would love the chance to continue to make her life miserable. She sat by her attorney, who was still going over her file. Tarik was talking to Sharice. He noticed Katrina and began talking loudly for her benefit.

"If she thinks that I'm going to just lie down and let her have anything to do with my kids, then she has another think coming. I won't allow my babies around a good-for-nothing whore." Katrina ignored him. Mr. Sloane said to him,

"Lower your voice, young man; can't you see all these people around?"

"Who are you?" Tarik asked. Mr. Sloane didn't answer him. "That's what I thought. You need to mind your business, old man." Tarik looked at Katrina and said,

"You know that I'll be asking the judge to terminate your parental rights permanently, don't you?" Katrina didn't say anything.

Mr. Sloane stood up, looked Tarik straight in the eye, and said, "Well young man, we will just have to see about that."

Tarik, angered by Mr. Sloane said, "Now here you go again old man, all up in my business. As I asked you before, who are you?"

"I'm Harold Sloane, Ms. McAllister's attorney."

Tarik stepped back out of respect and fear. "The Harold Sloane? Are you the owner of The Harolco Corporation?"

"Not that it's any of your business, but, yes, I am." Mr. Sloane said.

Tarik turned his attention to Katrina. "I'm impressed Katrina. How did you manage to get him to represent you?" He looked at Mr. Sloane. "What favors did she do to get you to represent her?"

Mr. Sloane got in Tarik's face and said, "You watch your mouth young man. Now you listen here. I'm a man of integrity, and I don't appreciate what you are insinuating. Ms. McAllister is an incredibly beautiful person, and she's a good woman and has contributed a lot to this community." He turned his attention towards Katrina and said, "I didn't know it then, but after our first few meetings, I did a little research on you. Imagine my surprise when I found out that you were volunteering at Jehovah's Way. You didn't know it was mine because I do things in anonymity. I want to thank you for all those years of service and all the good seeds that you've sown towards our cause and for giving back to the community. That's why I'll be taking your case pro bono. I have your check right here in my briefcase." Mr. Sloane handed Katrina her check. He never even deposited it. "Even if I hadn't found out about your working at the shelter, given all that you had been through, I still decided that I wasn't going to charge you."

"Oh Mr. Sloane, thank you. I didn't know that you owned Jehovah's Way."

"I know you didn't know; nobody knew except a few. I want you to know that I will stop at nothing to help you get your kids back. Don't you worry about a thing."

Tarik blurted out, "Alright old man, I don't care who you are. She ain't getting my kids. I've got a team of lawyers and judges who will crush you in court!" Mr. Sloane smiled and walked away. Katrina followed him. They all went into the courtroom. The bailiff walked towards the front of the courtroom and announced, "*All Rise! The Honorable Walter Griffin is in court.* Tarik looked at the judge in shock. He had no idea who he was. He leaned in and asked his attorney,

"Where in the hell is my judge?" She shrugged her shoulders and said,

"Don't worry, I got this."

His attorney tried every trick in the book, but she was unsuccessful. The judge sided with Katrina, and he found Tarik in contempt of court and reprimanded him for not following the court order and not allowing her to see her children. He even lectured him on the importance of the role of a mother in her children's lives and he apologized to Katrina for all that she had been through. He ordered that her children be allowed to see her immediately. Tarik was to take the children to her the following weekend. Katrina thanked the judge and hugged her attorney. While she was leaving the courtroom, Tarik mouthed the words, *"It ain't over bitch!"* She smiled and walked away. She was on top of the world and was not at all intimidated by his pathetic attempt to threaten her. He, in true fashion of a momma's boy, immediately got on the phone and called his mother, telling her about court.

"Mother, what happened to Judge Peters? He wasn't in court today. We had another judge who gave this girl visitation rights to my kids."

"Who was the judge?"

"Somebody named Walter Griffin."

"Okay, I'll get somebody on it right away," his mother said.

"Okay, and another thing, Mom, she got herself an attorney."

"She probably has some cheap-assed inexperienced attorney fresh out of law school. I wouldn't worry too much about that. Our attorneys will eat him alive. Or he can be bought just like the rest of them."

"I don't think so."

"What do you mean?"

Well, her attorney is Harold Sloane.

"Harold Sloane? You mean Harold Sloane from Sloane and Associates?"

"Yes, Mother, that Harold Sloane."

"How did she manage to get him?"

"Well, it seems she has done some work for him before. You know that she has been working at his homeless shelter. Do you know the building that you have been trying to get downtown? You know, Jehovah's Way. It's his." At that moment, Mrs. McAllister began to get a little worried. She knew that there was no chance of her getting that building, and although she had plenty of influence in that town, Harold Sloane Sr. had as much influence among an elite group of politicians and citizens who had refused to bow down to her and her antics.

"Don't you worry about anything; I'll take care of it." Although she asked Tarik not to worry, she *was* worried.

As Katrina was walking to her vehicle, Harold Jr. called her.

"Dad just called me a few minutes ago. He told me court was over. How did things go today?"

"Everything went great. Your dad was amazing, you should've been there! The judge sided in our favor. I get to see my babies this weekend."

"Congratulations! Would you have dinner with me tonight?"

"Yes, I will," she said feeling enthusiastic.

"Well, I'll be sending a car for you. Can you be ready by seven-thirty?"

"I can," she said.

"I can't wait to see you." He told her.

"I'm looking forward to it myself." Harold smiled to himself. He was glad that she had accepted his invitation once again.

"I'll see you later on," he said. She was so excited. Just a month ago, her life was totally different, but now things were looking up for her. She couldn't wait to get home. She went into her room, got her Bible, and read it for a while. She fell to her knees and prayed. She thanked God for what was taking place in her life.

Harold called. "I will be sending the car over for you thirty minutes early."

"Okay," she said. They chatted for a few minutes and Katrina got off the phone and got dressed. As he promised, the car was outside waiting for her. She checked her make-up and went to the car. The driver opened the door for her. She hurriedly got into the vehicle. Harold was already sitting inside, wearing a tuxedo and holding an orchid. Katrina was helped into the vehicle. She was surprised to see Harold. He presented her with the orchid. She took it and smiled. He kissed her on the cheek.

"Show off!"

"Hey, you can't knock a guy for trying, can you?" The driver pulled away from the curb and continued his route. He parked outside a small fancy boutique. Harold escorted Katrina inside, where a kind elderly black lady assisted her. She was dressed in a nice pantsuit. Her make-up was flawless, and she donned flashy rings on her fingers. She looked very stylish and confident. She stood straight and proud and gave Katrina a gentle handshake. "Hello lovely lady," she said, greeting Katrina. "Hello, ma'am."

"I'm Gloria and I'm here to assist you this evening."

"Thank you, Ms. Gloria. I'm Katrina."

"It's nice to meet you, Katrina. From what I understand, this young man would like for me to give you a glam touch this evening. With your lovely face and body type, that's going to be easy. I have many different styles that would look amazing on you. Come, follow me." Harold stood in the background, looking handsome as ever, smiling as the woman escorted Katrina away. He took a few phone calls as he patiently waited for her. Katrina was asked to pick out what she wanted to wear for the evening. She picked out a glamorous deep blue evening gown. She was fitted in a gorgeous set of five-inch heels that matched perfectly. Her soft, long, hair was pinned up in a glamorous ponytail with long curls cascading downward in a waterfall fashion. There was a crystal band pinned in front of her hair. She was wearing a glamorous sapphire necklace with a matching bracelet. Katrina walked back to where Harold was sitting. He was speechless. He walked up to Katrina and kissed her on the cheek. He then went over to the elderly clerk and hugged her.

"Thank you, Aunt Gloria! You've worked your magic. You've put a special touch on what was already a masterpiece. Isn't she beautiful Auntie?"

"She is lovely, and she is a very sweet young lady," his Aunt said. He reached into his jacket pocket and pulled out a small box. He opened the box; "Would you do me the honor of wearing this tonight?" It was a beautiful pair of diamond earrings. His aunt helped her put them on. She felt special. Harold gave her an adoring look and took her by the hand. "You two enjoy your evening," his aunt yelled as they exited the boutique and got back into the car. The driver drove them to the airport. He pulled up to a private jet, and they boarded. Katrina's mouth fell open.

"Harold, what are you doing?

"We're going to dinner." They boarded the plane.

"Where are we headed?"

"We are headed to Atlanta."

"Atlanta? Now you're really being a showoff with the limousine, the clothes, and the jet. I'm impressed, but why so much?"

"Because you're worth it. Now, can we enjoy our evening?" Katrina smiled and sat back in her seat. A young female flight attendant brought champagne and fruit over for them. Katrina was enjoying herself and she was enjoying all the attention that Harold was paying her. He made her feel special. When their jet landed, there was another limo waiting for them and whisked them away to an upscale restaurant. The place was closed to the public but there was an entire staff on hand waiting on them. A tall, thin, white gentleman dressed in a tuxedo was waiting for them and escorted them to their seat. A small jazz band was there playing music for them as they entered. "Wow, Harold. This is amazing. I love it," she said.

"I hope you do. You are a beautiful person, and you deserve all of this and more."

"How did you manage to get this beautiful restaurant?"

"It was easy," he said. "I own it."

"Well, that'll do it!" They both laughed. After enjoying a long, intimate evening, he said, "I have a condo here in Atlanta; would you like to stay here tonight, or would you like to fly back home? You'll have your own room of course."

"I don't see any reason to rush back tonight." After dinner, the driver drove them to his condo. Katrina was taken in by his kindness and generosity. He reassured her that he was interested in her romantically. He placed his hand on her chin as she sat on the sofa. Gently lifting her head, he leaned in and kissed her on the lips. As she gave in to the kiss, her heart raced. She felt herself wanting him. She pulled back a little to gain her composure. "What's wrong?" She looked into his eyes and smiled and said, "Is this too good to be true?"

"That's what I keep asking myself," he said. His response made her want him more. They shared a passionate kiss. They enjoyed each other's company until bedtime. He escorted her to the bedroom that she would be sleeping in for the night. He stood by the door not wanting to leave. They embraced and shared another kiss. They reluctantly pulled away, and he went to his room with a smile. She went into her room and said, *"Wow God, you really did a good job with that one."* She laughed to herself and tried to go to sleep. The following morning, Katrina was awakened by a gentle knock on the door.

"Hi Katrina, may I come in?" It was Harold. Katrina pulled the covers up to her chest and said, "Yes come in." He walked in the door looking wide awake. He rushed to her bedside. "Good morning beautiful," he said as he kissed her on the forehead.

"Good morning. You look awfully chipper this morning?"

"If you were in my shoes, you'd be happy too," he said. "Did you know you're just as beautiful freshly awakened?"

"Look at you, laying it on thick this morning," she said smiling.

"I have a surprise for you today."

"You mean more than last night?" She exhaled.

"I don't think I can take any more surprises."

"I had your things brought in from the car last night. I know you didn't want to wear that evening gown on our shopping trip today. When you get dressed, we'll have breakfast, and we'll go shopping after that. We need to get you some clothes to wear for lunch today"

"Harold, you don't have to do all of that."

"Stop that. Get dressed so we can hang out today." He kissed her again and left the room. She sprung out of bed like a little girl on her birthday and got showered and dressed. They ate breakfast, and afterwards, he had his driver take them all over the city. It was around three in the afternoon, and they were done. Katrina was exhausted. She never knew she could be that exhausted from having a great time. They went back to Harold's condo where she went in and showered. They met back in the living quarters. She sat next to him. He took her feet and placed them on his lap. He gently massaged them as they talked.

"Are you ready to go home?"

"If you were me, would you be ready? She laughed.

"I'm not ready to take you back."

"I'm not ready to leave." They began kissing. This time more passionately than ever. Things were getting so heated, that the temptation to allow things to go further was apparent. She wanted him. She wanted to feel him inside of her. She imagined him going all the way as she fed him her tongue. She craved his body, but again, they resisted the urge and chose to follow their hearts and not their bodies. She scooted over, adding a little space between them.

"You know, Harold, I didn't think I could ever feel this way again. I told myself that I would never allow myself to fall in love again. It was too much pain associated with loving someone."

"If it's causing you pain then it's not love. I don't understand how a man could ever hurt you. You're God's daughter and you should be treated with love and care and the kindness that a man should have for a woman. Only a savage beast would lay hands on a woman. I tell you, I get angry at the thought of the pain you've endured at his hands. I want to show you how a lady should be treated. I want to give you everything that you deserve. A man should cherish and bestow love upon a woman, not pain or force of will. I understand that your wounds are raw, but I can't help but feel a connection with you. I'm overwhelmed by your very presence. If you would only allow for nature and God's grace to steer our course, I feel we could have something awe-inspiring." I want you, Katrina. I want to cherish you in every way. I want you to think one day of becoming my lady." Katrina was speechless. She didn't know how to respond. She leaned in and kissed him. She moved over to him and laid her head on his shoulder. Tears streamed down her cheeks. He held her and allowed her to cry. He comforted her and spoke kindly to her encouraging her to let it all out. She cried until she fell asleep in his arms. He prayed for her as she slept. He prayed for her inner healing and any physical healing that she needed. Although he had not met them, he prayed for her children. He ended his prayer by silently asking God to allow him to be her mate and to show him how to help her with the healing process in her life. He could tell that she had been damaged, and he wanted to take her pain away. After praying for her, he too fell asleep. They went home the following day.

Visitation Day

Katrina was rushing through the house with nervous excitement. It was almost time for her to see her children. Tarik had been ordered to surrender the children for visitation. A court liaison was assigned to the case to ensure that he obeyed the court order. The liaison, along with Katrina's attorney, was at Katrina's home waiting on Tarik. Meanwhile, back at the McAllister mansion, Tarik was gathering the kids for their visit with their mother.

"Alexis, TJ, come here for a minute. We have a visit with your mom soon." The kids were excited.

"Oh yes, mommy!" Alexis said jumping up and down with excitement. Tarik was irritated and warned her.

"You will not be staying. You're only visiting for the weekend. Your mom is very sick right now, and she won't be able to see you guys much longer after this visit. She doesn't love you as much as I do. She's going away for a long time, and you're going to have a new mommy—a real mommy, a mommy who loves you.

Alexis said, "I don't want a new mommy! I love my mommy!" She began to cry, and Tarik scolded her.

"Hush if you know what's good for you."

TJ was afraid for his sister and said, "Yeah Alexis, be quiet." TJ comforted his sister.

"Leave her alone TJ. She's going to have to learn that she can't have everything her way. Your momma had her spoiled. But we're going to change all of that. Alexis began crying again. Mrs. McAllister walked into the room talking on her cell phone. "Look Mayor, this family has contributed thousands of dollars to your campaign. Not to mention the many favors that you needed. And you're telling me that you'll try? Look here your Honor, make something happen! I want that building and I want it now. I don't care who owns it. I did not come this far to let something like another homeless shelter stop me. Do it now!" Abruptly hanging up the phone, she looked at Tarik and the kids. Alexis was still crying softly.

"Oh Lord, not this again! Tarik, what is she crying for now? I don't have time for this today. Please get them out of here!"

"She's a little upset right now, but she'll be alright real soon, once she gets her new stepmom. Isn't that right, baby girl?" Alexis refused to answer her father. He asked her again. "Isn't that right baby girl?" he said louder in a threatening tone.

"Yes sir."

"Alright now, that's better. Now go and hug your grandmother and tell Mandy I said to get you dressed." The kids tried to hug their grandmother. She barely hugged them. They left the room. "Have you and Sharice set a date yet because I'm sick and tired of those little brats? They're all over the place. And that little Alexis, I swear she's going to turn out just like her mother with those nasty ways of hers."

"She'll be alright. She's just missing Katrina right now. After this little visit this weekend, we'll get Judge Peters back on this case and we'll terminate her rights to the children for good. Sharice and I are having dinner tonight. We'll discuss a wedding date at that time."

"Well hurry it along. Sharice is a good girl who comes from a great family with good moral values. I'm looking forward to her being in the family. And; besides, once you two get married, the judge will have no choice but to take those kids from Katrina for good."

"Could you try not to sound so excited about all of this? And you're not fooling anybody, you don't like Sharice. You just like her because her family is worth millions, and you want this big merger to go through with her dad's company."

"Boy, don't you sass me! Besides, you must admit, it feels better to marry someone worth something than some no-good, poor, street trash like Katrina. She tried to trap you by having those babies. She thought that she would have a couple of kids, and she would be set for life. But we're going to fix that real soon. She will not get those kids or one thin dime of the McAllister's fortune." Mrs. McAllister pressed the intercom. "Mandy, get me a gin and tonic now."

Tarik arrived with the kids as instructed. Katrina was standing in the doorway anxiously waiting. When she saw her babies coming down the walkway, she was overcome with emotion. Her eyes welled up with tears and she ran to her children. Alexis screamed. "Mommy!" TJ held his mother so long, that he was afraid to let go. They clung to each other as they walked into the house. Everyone was in tears, including the court liaison. After the children were settled in, the court liaison asked the children and Katrina a few questions. She then spoke with Mr. Sloane and she and Mr. Sloane left. The children got settled in, and they refused to leave their mother's side. Harold called Katrina and told her that he wanted to let her use the car and the jet for the weekend. He offered for her to take her children anywhere they wanted to go. She accepted his offer providing he'd join them. He responded by saying,

"Katrina, I don't want to intrude on this visit. You need this time for you and your babies. I'll stop by on Sunday to meet them. In the meantime, I want you all to enjoy yourself this weekend."

She wasn't sure if she could take the children out of the state, so rather than doing that, she took them to a famous ice cream shop and extravagant kid stores in the state, traveling to two major cities. They enjoyed their weekend together. The weekend seemed too short. Sunday came and the children were to leave at six that evening. Chandra and her mother prepared a special dinner for everyone. They invited Mr. Sloane to eat with them. He was on hand as her attorney to ensure that the exchange of the children went according to the court order. Harold came to dinner to meet the children and the rest of the family and to lend Katrina his support. They ate dinner and had a great time. Chandra and their mother were mesmerized by Harold. Their mother was amazed at how well he knew about the bible. They talked so much about the Lord, that His presence filled the atmosphere. Everyone laughed and talked, and the children were at peace. They knew they were in a good place where they were loved and not pushed aside like at the McAllister mansion. Everyone doted on the children and all the adults listened to them. TJ and Harold were like two peas in a pod. Tarik never dedicated the time his children needed. TJ shared his passion with Harold, which was his love of math, science, and playing the guitar. Alexis was enjoying herself. Everyone was enjoying a beautiful evening. The doorbell rang and everybody's heart sank. They knew who it was. There was silence as Chandra went to the door. It was Tarik. He was a couple of hours early. Everyone began to head towards the living room. Katrina said, "You're a little early. We weren't expecting you for a couple of hours."

"Well, I have some important business to take care of, and it can't wait, so I had to come a little early."

"Our time is not up! We were just having dinner. Can you come back? "No, I can't come back. The judge said you were supposed to get them for the weekend, and I did that, now it's time for them to go. A couple of hours won't make a bit of difference." Mr. Sloane walked in and confronted him. "Ms. McAllister's visitation is not over yet. Tarik was getting upset. He began to direct his anger towards Katrina in the hopes of intimidating her.

"Why is your last name still McAllister? Why didn't you change it after the divorce? You're not a McAllister anymore. Why are you still holding on to my name? You wish you were still married to me, don't you? But you're not."

Harold walked up behind his father and Katrina and interrupted Tarik.

"Oh, trust me; that's all going to change soon." Katrina and Harold look at each other passionately. Tarik noticed, and he was annoyed by the joy in Katrina's heart and the smile on her face. He snarled,

"She ain't nothing but used trash, my leftovers. I don't see what you see in her."

Harold had heard enough. He could no longer hold his peace. He gently moved Katrina behind him and got directly in Tarik's face.

"I understand that you have kids with Katrina, and for that reason alone, the two of you must have contact." Tarik tried to interrupt but Harold stopped him.

"No, let me finish." Harold continued, "Now this is an amazing woman and hopefully one day soon, she'll be my wife."

"Well, I feel sorry for you. You can have my trash," Tarik said with a halfhearted grin. "I will not stand here and allow you to disrespect or demean her in my presence. I care for her, and I'll thank God every day for blessing me with her."

Katrina could hardly contain her pride. At that very moment, she felt love for Harold, and it was then that she knew they were meant to be. Harold continued speaking.

"I'll say this, and I'll be done. You had your chance, and you blew it. Now that you feel that you couldn't break her when you had her, you're not complete. Get over it, your time has passed. Move on. You call this beautiful woman, the mother of *your* children trash? She may be trash to you, but to me, she's a real treasure. Her worth is priceless. You stand there trying to insult her but you're only insulting yourself. I don't see how you can call yourself a man. You're showing your ignorance. You had treasure right in your hands, but you couldn't see it. You're childish and selfish. You're intimidated by her beautiful spirit. You knew that you didn't compare with such a magnificent lady. You were so afraid of losing her that you had to use fear and dominance to try and control her. You threatened her with her children using her love for them against her. You knew she couldn't possibly love you after all you had done, so the only way to keep her was through constant manipulation. As if that weren't enough, you used threats and violence to force her to stay. Looks like the sign of a desperate man to me. Pretty pathetic of you huh? It pains me to think of all the abuse she had to endure at your hands. I'm glad that you're no longer with her because you don't deserve a woman like her. You act as if you don't want her but we both know that you do. Being a man of wealth, you should've recognized this precious and rare jewel. It's your loss. Oh, and another thing; you will not use the children to try to control her. You could care less about those babies, but I can see that it's your last-ditch effort to try and hold on to Katrina. Just let it go, you spoiled brat. It's over. Move on with your life." Feeling a bit intimidated, Tarik took a step backward as Harold continued to close the gap between them. With a determined gaze, Harold stared him down. He almost wanted Tarik to make a move so he could give him the beating he deserved but he refrained as he knew violence wasn't the answer. Not on this day but he was prepared to protect Katrina and the children.

"What do I want with her? I am about to be married to the richest most beautiful woman in this state.

"And I feel sorry for her," Harold said.

"I'm no longer afraid of you Tarik," Katrina said. "You don't scare me anymore."

"Tarik put his hand up and said, "Whatever woman, go get my kids."

Mr. Sloane repeated himself. "Mr. McAllister, their visit is not over. Now you can either sit and wait patiently, or you can step outside and wait, but you will comply with the court order and allow them to complete their visit." Tarik, feeling defeated, left angrily. "I'll be in the car," he said. He stormed to his car like an upset toddler and called his mother while the children finished their visit. He was anxious to tell her what was happening. "Hello," his mother said answering. "Momma, I'm over here trying to pick up the kids and that damn attorney of hers will not allow me to get my children. I'm so angry. I ought to just go right in there and…"

"And what? She has no right to keep those kids beyond her allotted time."

"That's just it. They say her time isn't up yet; Mother, you need to hurry and get me a new judge. I can't take this." His mother retorted, "No, what you should've done was listen to me in the first place and not marry her, and you definitely shouldn't have had children with her. Now, this is your mess. If you want me to help you clean it up, then you're going to have to be patient. We'll get our judge, and we'll make her pay. I should've let you finish her off that day at the birthday party and made it look like an accident. At least we wouldn't be dealing with this crap now."

"Oh, Momma, another thing, do you care to guess who she's seeing now?"

"Who?"

"She's dating Harold Sloane Jr. He said he's going to marry her."

"Well, doesn't our little whore get around! She's managed to snag herself another gullible rich young man. What in the hell do you men see in her?" Tarik's mind began to wander. He could easily answer her question. He knew what Harold saw in Katrina, and quite frankly, he was jealous of the thought of the two of them being together. He was even more troubled that Katrina was enjoying her life without him. Another man was now appreciating her, making her smile, and protecting her. Something he'd lost sight of. He secretly loved her all along. She was beautiful to him, and he had been obsessed with her. He was always afraid of losing her. He tried to imprison her due to his fears. He never intended for her to leave him. He thought he would always maintain control over her. He was under pressure from his mother. He chose to have an affair with Sharice, a woman whom he didn't love, but it pleased his mother, who was in it for the money. He knew deep down that he had allowed his jealousy to get the best of him when dealing with his wife. He was aware that he would one day lose her. He had gone so far with the abuse, and his anger and jealousy had taken control of him, he felt he couldn't stop. When Katrina stopped fighting back, it gave him a false sense of pride and it fed his ego. When she left home, he was devastated but he couldn't let anyone know. He missed her. His mother handled the divorce and the politics around Katrina not receiving custody of the kids or the McAllister money. Now that Katrina's life was back on track, he saw her as he once did when they were younger. She was more beautiful than he could ever remember. He's heartbroken now that she's dating Harold Jr. He remembered the love that he felt when he first saw her. How he wished for a moment that he could turn back the hands of time. It was too late for that; too much damage had been done, and too much time had passed. Sitting silently in his thoughts, a tear fell from his face.

"Tarik! Are you still there?" He cleared his throat saying,

"Yes momma, I'm here."

"I need to go. I have to call Sharice." Tarik wasn't going to call Sharice. He needed a little time to gather his thoughts.

"Well, tell her I said hello."

"I will." He started his engine and drove around town for a couple of hours sulking. He knew that he was the cause of all that was happening. He felt a sense of regret that he hadn't been man enough to stand up to his mother when it came to his marriage. Not only did she run his life, but she had a major hold on his father as well. His mother had emasculated his father, and she had major control over every aspect of their lives. It was because of his mother that they were rich. She had taken his grandmother's small business, which was barely thriving, and turned it into the major company it is today. Mrs. McAllister's mother had come from a well-to-do family, and her parents died in a car crash when she was eighteen years old, leaving her everything. It only fueled her selfish behavior. She raised her son with the same elitist attitude she had. Tarik was driving all over town trying to get the image of his ex-wife with another man out of his head. He felt embarrassed about his futile attempt to intimidate her. He knows she has a real chance of defeating him in court. She was standing up to him and that was something she'd never done before. He almost felt a sense of dread going back to pick up the children. It was he who was now intimidated. Without his mother there to support him, he had to face Katrina and her supporters alone. He drove back over but he decided not to go inside. He simply blew his horn like a coward and Katrina escorted her children out to the car. The children didn't want to leave. Alexis was taking it hard. "Mommy I don't want to go!"

"Me neither," said TJ. Tarik was sitting in the car impatiently waiting. The children were hesitant about getting in the car dragging themselves slowly along.

"Mommy will see you again next weekend sweetheart," Katrina told her.

"But Mommy, I don't want to go. She grabbed Katrina's leg as she tried to walk her to the car. "You have to go with Daddy, sweetie." TJ held his mother around the waist. "Momma please, don't make us go back."

"You have to according to the judge. But Mommy will see you in just a few days ok." Tarik, watching what was going on, had to get out of the car and physically pull Alexis and TJ away from Katrina. She and the children were very emotional. It was hard seeing them go. Harold came outdoors just as Tarik was pulling away. Katrina leaned on him for support. He held her as she cried. "It's going to be alright. Dad will stop at nothing to make sure they're home for good. Just wait and see. You deserve to be with your children and God wants you to have them." He continued to comfort her. They walked back towards the home. Mr. Sloane sat with the family and shared the strategy he would use in court. After the brief meeting, he excused himself and left. Harold requested that Katrina leave with him. He knew it was a difficult time for her, so he didn't want her to be alone. They said their goodbyes to Chandra and her mother, and they left.

Chapter Eight

Harold and Katrina went to breakfast. She was still emotional thinking about the children. She was picking over her breakfast hardly eating.

"Honey, are you okay?"

She shook it off and said, "I'm sorry, I was just thinking about my babies. You should've seen the look on their faces. It was all I could do to keep from breaking down."

"I understand love." Harold reached across the table and gently took her hand. "Katrina, I want to know if you would do me a favor."

"What is it?"

"I have a condo that's not being occupied. It hasn't been lived in a couple of years. I only visit now and then. I had intentions of selling it, but I always felt that I needed to hold on to it. I want you to move into it."

"You want me to move into your condo?"

"Yes, I want you to think of it as your permanent residence. When you go to court, the judge is going to want to know where you're living. You need to show that you have a permanent residence of your own to regain custody of your children. Dad also wanted me to ask if you would consider becoming director of his affairs at Jehovah's Way shelter. You'll receive ample pay with benefits."

"I don't believe this! Are you serious?"

"Yes, I'm serious. You did such a wonderful job when you were volunteering all those years. We believe you're the perfect person for the position. Also, it'll look good when you go to court. It won't look like it's staged because you had been volunteering there for years anyway."

"Harold, I think that's a great idea! I don't know what to say."

"There's only one thing that you should say."

"Yes, of course, I will," she said. She removed herself from her seat and went around to Harold and hugged him while he was still sitting. He smiled. He gently pulled her by the waist and sat her on his lap. They shared a kiss. Katrina's spirits were lifted by the news.

"Finish your breakfast and we'll go there."

"I'm too excited to eat; let's go now," she said with all the eagerness of a teen girl getting her first car. They left and drove over to his condo. Once there, she could hardly wait for the vehicle to stop before jumping out.

"Harold it is fabulous! Are you sure about this?" Katrina asked.

"Of course, I'm sure."

She walked through the two-story mini-mansion of the fully furnished condo. Every room was filled with extravagant items, including expensive art collections and out-of-this-world décor.

"Wow. Did you decorate this yourself?"

"I hired an interior decorator for most of it, but my mom and aunt did the rest. There's a Range Rover in the garage. It's yours to drive. No lady of mine will be seen driving that little bug of a car you have." Katrina looked at him.

"Lady?" He took her hand and pulled her close.

"Yes, I said lady. Will you be my lady?" Before she could give him an answer, he covered her mouth with his lips. She was lost in his kiss as he gently embraced her. Her heart raced and her belly shuttered. She went limp in his arms. Her spirit soared. She was in love. She was sure of it.

"Yes," she answered in between kisses. He took her by the hand and led her through the condo. "There's plenty of space for the children to play. It also comes with a housekeeper and a chef. You will need someone to clean it and with your busy schedule, I'm sure you could make use of the chef's services when needed. No lady of mine..." She kissed him before he could get it out." "I know" They laughed. He took her to the vehicle that he had for her to drive and gave her the keys. He also gave her two credit cards of her own. If you need anything, let me know. I'm your man now and I want you to have the best of everything. What's mine is yours."

"I'm overwhelmed, Harold. I don't know what to say."

"Katrina, I love you. I desire you. I know that it seems as if I'm moving too fast but why wait? I'm a man and I know what I want."

"She expressed her feelings for him as well."

Harold reached inside his shirt pocket.

"I've been holding on to this for a few days now. I wanted to give it to you last week but now seems to be the right time to present it to you." He took out a ring and said, "I want to give you this ring as a token of our friendship and our love. He placed a three-carat princess-cut diamond solitaire on her right hand. "It's so pretty Harold."

"Nothing can compare to your beauty." He kissed her again and said, "As much as I would love to stay here with you, I have a hectic schedule today. Here are your keys. The code is on the card inside and I've already called to make plans to have your things moved here. Do everything you can to get settled in. What are you going to do with your old car?"

"I'm going to take it to my sister's place for now."

"No, I'll have someone do it for you. Don't stress about it." Katrina, still taking in the entirety of the moment said,

"I...I don't know what to say. I'm speechless. This is all so much."

"I know it's a lot to take in, but you deserve this and so much more. Now you can relax and focus on the children. I don't want you stressing about a thing. When I get home this evening, I'll call you, and perhaps you can come over to my place for dinner, or we can go out if you'd like."

"That would be great."

"Go and get settled in and make it comfortable for you. I love you." Harold kissed Katrina and left. She was standing in the doorway of her new place. She was in awe. She immediately began to thank God. *"When you say you're going to bless someone, you really do it big don't you?* She smiled while gripping her keys and then she ran through the place like a little child on Christmas morning. She looked in every room; she went out back to admire the pool. Looking in each room was an adventure for her. The place was lovely, and it was hers. She used the day to get settled in. There was really nothing she had at her sister's place of value but her photographs and her bible. She got in her new vehicle and drove back to Chandra's to get a few of her things.

Chandra was at work, but her mother was home. She told her mother all that happened. "I'm so happy for you Katrina. When God moves, he sure does move quickly doesn't he?"

"Yes Mom, and until I saw it with my own eyes, I had all but lost hope. I can't believe I spent my adult life not believing in Him. Since I was going through so much hell, I felt He didn't love me or didn't exist. But look at Him now. I tell you I believe in Him now! I have a chance at getting my children; a great man who adores me, is looking out for me, and loves God. I have a new job running the entire business of the Jehovah's Way shelter for my attorney and a new home. God is real."

"Yes, he is," her mother said. She hugged Katrina. "I'm happy that you're happy."

"Thank you, Mom." Katrina went into her bedroom, gathered the few things she wanted, and placed them in her vehicle. She said goodbye to her mother and left. She went shopping for new clothes for her new job and her court appearance and she also shopped for the children. She also picked up a few beautiful garments to go out on dates with Harold. She drove back to the condo and put everything up. She got settled in, called her sister, and invited her over. Chandra was excited to see her new place. She came right over after work. Chandra walked through the door. She was flabbergasted.

"Ooh girl, you have got to be kidding me! Is this where you're going to be living? Talk about moving on up, you did it big time." Chandra noticed her ring. "Girl, look at the rock on your finger. Has he proposed already?"

"This is a friendship ring. But it's gorgeous. He also gave me a couple of credit cards with no limits on them."

"Are you serious?"

"Yes, and his father has hired me to run the shelter. Oh, and did you see that vehicle out there? It's mine too." They both screamed with excitement. "Since I'm going to be running his entire operation over at Jehovah's Way shelter, I'm going to need an assistant so guess who I was considering for the position?"

"Who girl?"

"You of course, who else? I just need a little time to go in and see where I can place you, but I want you to resign from your job and come and work alongside me. You've been complaining about that place long enough. They don't deserve you anyway. You may not have been in a position to quit, and I understand that but now you can tell them where to go. After the many years you've given them, they failed to give you decent promotions. Working with me will double, almost triple your pay and you can finally take some time for yourself and a much-needed vacation."

"I would love that. I'll need to give my job notice and I have a pension plan and other benefits that I'll be receiving. So, let me know when you're ready."

"I will." Katrina paused for a second and looked at her sister. "I'm falling in love with him sis. He wants so badly to protect me. I know he cares about me, but sometimes I can't help but ask myself, will it last."

"Girl, you are dealing with a different type of person than Tarik. I hate to even mention him and Harold in the same sentence. It feels like an abomination to do so. Harold is a hard worker, a man of God, and he helped his parents when he could've gone out on his own. He's a family man. He needs you just as much as you need him. God knew what he was doing when he put that man in your life. I can tell how he looks at you, the way that he cared for you during dinner the other day, how much he adores you. He was so protective of you. Oh, and I loved the way he stood up for you against Tarik. Girl, Tarik was too through. He ran away like a scared little boy."

"He did that didn't he?" Katrina smiled thinking about it.

"Girl, I wanted to scream with joy! Mom and I were peeking from the dining room, cheering him on. You already know Mom was in there waiting for something to pop off; she had her purse ready."

"Girl, what are we going to do about that old lady?"

"She loves us; she shows it in unconventional ways at times, but I feel her love. As far as Harold is concerned, I like him. It's alright to be a little guarded, and I can understand why, given your past, but I want you to let go of the past and the negative thoughts. Enjoy your life. You deserve it."

Katrina's phone rang. It was Harold calling. She answered, and they spoke for a few minutes. While she was doing that, Chandra continued to admire her new place. Katrina walked back to where her sister was standing. "That was Harold. He's picking me up for dinner tonight. Come on, let me show you what I plan on wearing." The two of them laughed and talked until close to the time for Katrina to leave. After Chandra left, Katrina got dressed and went downstairs to wait for Harold. She noticed his car pulling into the driveway. She was surprised that he rang the doorbell instead of using his key. As she opened the door, Harold's face froze with delight. He was floored at how beautiful she looked. She stood wearing a lovely off-the-shoulder, shimmering red evening gown. She donned an exquisite ruby necklace, set in gold with diamonds surrounding the rubies with matching earrings. Her hair was in a curly ponytail atop her head. Her make-up was professionally done. He placed his hand over his heart and gasped the words, "Beautiful; you look amazing!" He kissed Katrina on the cheek. She got her clutch, and he escorted her to the car. On their way, he lovingly flirted with her, taking her by the hand he held until they reached their destination. Dinner was romantic, and Harold spared no expense when it came to wooing his love. His love for her grew stronger daily. The bond they began to share grew with each passing moment. Harold knew they were destined to be together. He requested that she come to dinner with his parents. He wanted to formally introduce her to his mother. Harold's not the kind of man who randomly brought women into his mother's presence. He was so smitten with his new love that he wanted to share her with his mother. Although his father and aunt knew about their love, he wanted his mother to share his joy. Harold's mother is a lovely woman. Well-loved in her community and was a beautiful socialite. She was always involved in something positive in the community. She refused to grow old gracefully. The short but pudgy, fair-skinned woman enjoyed her husband and her life. Harold felt that she and Katrina would love one another, and he was right. Once he introduced Katrina to his mother, they became closer, and they began spending time together. She was the daughter she never had. Everything was looking up for Katrina. Her visits with her children continued. The children loved spending time with Harold and Katrina. Katrina was working daily at the shelter division. She hired her sister to work alongside her as her assistant. It'd been close to eight months since Harold and Katrina's first encounter. A lot had happened in such a short time. Unbeknownst to Katrina and Harold, Mr. Sloane hired a private investigator to investigate the McAllisters. Because the statute of limitations had not yet run out, Mr. Sloane requested that all the information on Katrina's assault case be reopened. He had the state investigators come in to oversee the case because of rumors of wrongdoing within the local police department. Detective John Akers, the original detective on the case, was more than willing to assist Mr. Sloane, so he provided all the evidence that he'd collected and saved. Mr. Sloane also had another judge investigate her divorce decree and the order on it. It was puzzling to the court that a woman could be married to a man for many years without having a prenuptial agreement and end up not getting a single dime or sole or even shared custody of her children when she had not been proven to be an unfit parent. A thorough investigation into Tarik's finances was ordered. Little did Mr. Sloane know that by doing so, they would uncover a trail of corruption. An immediate investigation was carried out into his parents as well as anybody with whom they did business. The investigation yielded findings of corruption that went back to the late seventies up to the present day. It didn't take long for the information to hit the media. The McAllister family, who regularly enjoyed the spotlight and media attention, soon found themselves hiding out from the unwanted attention. Their business contacts and most of their friends wanted nothing to do with them. Most of them had already been under investigation by the Internal Revenue Service and other federal agencies. Indictments were coming down faster than rain showers in April—bribery, corruption, wrong-doing, cover-ups, and lying to a federal grand jury. The mayor, judges, chief of police, and their attorneys were all indicted. Any and everybody in that town who was negatively affected by the McAllisters came running to tell their stories. Their employees were selling them out faster than expensive items at a cheap auction. Katrina was awarded temporary custody of TJ and Alexis, and chances were pretty good that she would be gaining full custody of them; it was merely a matter of the proper paperwork and the judge.

As life continually got worse for the McAllister family, it had gotten that much better for Katrina. She had a whole new life, far different from the one in which she lived before. Things were going great for her. Tarik was finally in jail on numerous charges, including an assault charge for the attack on Katrina. He sent word for her to come to visit him. She decided to go and see him. Chandra went with her. Neither of them knew what he wanted, but she went for the children's sake. The guards escorted her to the area where he was waiting. She walked in and saw him in an orange jumpsuit. She couldn't believe her eyes. He looked far different from the man who used to torment her. He had grown a full beard. His hair was in thick, massive lumps all over his head. He looked like a street thug with no grooming. She hardly recognized him. He appeared very humble. He motioned for her to sit down. He spoke in a very mild tone. Katrina didn't know what to think of his behavior. She took her seat, keeping her eyes on him. Chandra stood in the background as they visited.

"I'm glad you came," he said to Katrina.

"You sent word saying it was urgent."

"Yes, it is. I first want to start by saying that I apologize for everything I've done to you. I'm sorry for the horrible things I put you through. I know I wasn't a good husband. Being here these last few days has allowed me to reflect on my life and what I've done wrong. Katrina, we were both young when we first got married, and I wasn't mature enough to be a husband. I chose to listen to my mother rather than listen to my heart. She always hated the fact that I married you. I wanted her approval. It seems the only time she was ever really pleased with me was when I treated you harshly. The worse I treated you, the happier she became. She intended for me to marry Sharice, but I chose you instead. She was always driven by money. She felt that since your family had none, our relationship was futile. The woman she wanted me to marry has left

238

me. There will be no merger with her father's company. My mom made a lot of bad investments and was involved in illegal activities dating back to my birth. Our money and all our assets are frozen by the IRS. I can't even afford a good attorney at this point and will be forced to use a public defender. I'm going to lose custody of the kids for good." He began to sob.

"I've never gotten over our divorce. I'm still in love with you. Outside of our children, you meant the world to me. I didn't know how to show it. I wished I'd treated you the way you deserved. I'm so sorry for what I've done to you." He continued to cry.

"Do you think that you could ever find it in your heart to forgive me?" He reached for her hand.

She pulled back slightly and said, "You and your family were very cruel to me, and your mother was cruel to my children. At first, I found it exceedingly difficult to forgive you, especially given the years of torment you all put me through. After I began to read my bible, I realized that to be forgiven, I must forgive. Although I've not forgotten the pain you all inflicted on me and my children, I want you to know that I forgive you."

Tarik placed his hand on the back of Katrina's. She cringed at his touch.

"Thank you. I knew that you would forgive me. You have always had a good heart." Katrina looked at him feeling a bit disgusted.

He looked into her eyes and said, "I still love you, baby. I need to know if you would do me a favor."

"What is it?"

"I want to know if you could get your attorney to help me out and drop these assault and battery charges."

Chandra, who had been watching the entire time, looked up at that moment and asked, "Are you kidding? Do you think that my sister is a fool or something?"

"Chandra, why don't you mind your own business? This has nothing to do with you," Tarik said. Katrina looked at Chandra and said,

"Chandra, don't worry about me; I'm okay. Just give us a few minutes alone please." Feeling a bit alarmed Chandra was afraid that Tarik would convince Katrina to drop the charges against him.

"Sis, please tell me that you are not falling for this creep."

"Chandra please; leave us alone for a few minutes."

Tarik looked up at Chandra and said, "You heard her. Now leave us alone." Chandra reluctantly walked away. Katrina gently walked up to Tarik's chair, and she leaned toward him as if she were about to kiss him.

Tarik whispered to her, "I knew you couldn't say no to me. You've never been able to resist me. That's why I love you so much."

Katrina waved her finger in his face and said, "Look, you selfish, arrogant momma's boy! You acted like an animal and you'll be treated like one. These bars fit you nicely. Enjoy your cage! You tried to put me in a prison. You sentenced me to a life of abuse while we were together. You violated all of my basic human rights, and I allowed it because I loved my children. You blamed your mother for your abusing me. You've never taken full responsibility for your mischievous and evil deeds a day in your life. You'll never change. How could you sit here after all you've done to me and still think that I would help you? The only help I can give is a bible and a little advice. Don't drop the soap, Nigga!"

Katrina turned around to leave. As she was walking away Tarik yelled out, "Those are my kids you bitch! You better not put your slutty hands on them. When I get out of here, I'm coming for you!" Katrina turned around and walked up to his chair. She slapped him with so much force that he fell out of his chair. She walked away. Tarik yelled out to the guard.

"Guard, did you see that?" The guard turned her head as if she didn't hear him. As Katrina approached the door, the guard gave Katrina a fist bump as she walked out of the visitation room. Katrina and Chandra left.

"Can you believe that he called me down here to help him after all he and his family have done to me? I should've never wasted my time coming here. I should've known that he had an ulterior motive for requesting me."

"Girl, you had me scared there for a minute. You had that look in your eyes as if you were feeling sorry for him."

"Oh, I felt sorry for him, alright, but not in the way you were thinking."

"I like the way you slapped the mess out of him girl. I didn't think you had it in you."

"You should've heard how his head sounded when he hit the floor," Katrina said. They both laughed uncontrollably. "Girl, I have to go check on my babies."

"Okay," said Chandra.

"I'm headed to the house. I've got to go and get dinner started for me and Mom."

"Harold is coming over for dinner tonight. Why don't you and Mom come over? I'll have the chef add something extra for you two."

"Are you sure, sis? I don't want to impose on you guys."

"Girl, it's no problem. Go and get Mom, and you two come right on over. I'll tell Harold that you'll be joining us. He'll love it, and so will the kids."

"Okay, we will." Katrina got in her vehicle. On her way home, she began to smile thinking about what she had done to Tarik. She caught herself enjoying the moment. She thought about it again, and feeling a small sense of guilt, she prayed for a few minutes. *"Lord, forgive me for what I did to Tarik. I read in your word where you said vengeance is yours, you will repay. I can see where you're already working on my behalf. He just made me so upset by the way he talked to me."* After her brief prayer, she called Harold.

"Hi honey," she said to Harold. He was happy to hear from her. "I just want to inform you that Mom and Chandra will be joining us for dinner tonight. Is that okay with you?"

"Oh baby, you know you don't have to ask. I would be delighted to have dinner with them. Hey, what would your sister say if I brought one of my business partners along? It's not a blind date or anything. Your sister is quite lovely, and they're both single. He rarely gets out. I think it would be a great idea to introduce him to your sister. He's a genuinely nice guy. You've met him once at that banquet. Do you remember Dale Williamson?"

"Yes, I do, actually; he sat at our table."

"Yes, that's right," Harold said.

"What did you think of him?"

"I didn't focus on him all that much, but he was pretty nice. I don't think my sister would mind meeting him. Just bring him along, and we will let fate do the rest. I think that's a great idea honey."

"Perfect, we will be there in about an hour." Katrina hurried home to get her and the children ready for dinner. She called her sister and asked her to wear something pretty. Along with Chandra's beautiful spirit and personality, she had a beautiful face. She and Katrina look a lot alike. She was always taking care of others and their needs never really focusing on herself. Katrina knew it was a good idea to have the two meet. It was dinnertime and everyone was lounging around waiting for dinner to be served. Harold and his friend Dale finally arrived. Dale and Chandra seemed to hit it off nicely. They both needed this encounter and were grateful to their hosts for their connection. They sat next to each other at the dinner table. Laughter was heard by all, and everyone was enjoying themselves. After dinner, the children played video games while the adults talked. Dale was impressed with Chandra and she him. He wanted to see more of her, so they exchanged numbers before he left. The night was winding down and it was time for everyone to leave. Everyone said their goodbyes and Katrina went to read the children a bedtime story. After reading to them she talked to them about their grandparents and their father. From listening to her children, she could tell that they had been through a world of mental torment.

"Mommy, Daddy said you didn't love us anymore, and you left us," TJ said. Tarik tried to instill in the children that their mother had abandoned them and wanted nothing to do with them.

"Oh baby, that's not true. I love you both. One day, when you're older, I'll tell you everything, but for now, we're back together, and that's all that matters." After Katrina informed them that they would never have to live with Tarik or their grandparents, they told her everything that had been happening to them. TJ even recalled the assault that his dad committed on her. He remembered everything and not only had he seen most of the assaults that his dad did, but He was also able to recall them in great detail.

Alexis said, "Mommy, he was mean to you all the time. He was always fussing at you even when you were being a good mommy." The kids recalled many times that the McAllisters would speak of her negatively and call her names in front of the children. They told her of how their grandmother often yelled at them and how she was aggressive towards them. If she kept them, she would make them sit in one position for hours until Mandy came to get them for dinner. They went on and on about the horrible ways in which they were being treated. Katrina told them that they never had to worry about the McAllisters again. The children were relieved.

"We're a happy family, and you don't ever have to worry about going back to that bad place anymore," Katrina told them. They all slept in the same bed that night, and Katrina held her children and praised God.

Chapter Nine

Katrina enrolled her and the children in Christian counseling sessions to help them cope with the emotional trauma they endured. They were happy and healthy, and they were progressively getting better. They managed to put their troubles behind them. TJ was playing sports and taking guitar lessons while Alexis was into dancing and minor modeling. Katrina kept the children busy with activities they enjoyed. Their lives were vastly different from how they started. Harold was a father figure and a friend to the children and his parents were incredibly great hands-on grandparents for them. Chandra and Ruth were in their lives daily and everything was going great. Chandra and Dale were stable in their relationship and they were inseparable. There was even talk of marriage for the two. Katrina had sole custody of the children. After the McAllisters had exhausted all of their appeals and after all their crimes were tallied up, Frank and Francis each got a thirty-year mandatory sentence in the federal prison and were ordered to pay back millions in restitution. For the assault on Katrina, Tarik got fifteen years, and he got another twenty years in federal prison for his other crimes alongside his parents. He took the news very hard, and he ended his own life in his cell. Harold and Katrina were in place to make sure the children were okay after learning of their father's death. After a brief memorial service, the kids said their goodbyes in their way to their father. They didn't seem to be negatively affected by his passing. They went on with their little lives as if nothing had ever happened. Harold and Katrina were surprised, but given the hell that they had gone through, they could almost understand the children's reaction. Katrina did enroll them in grief counseling to ensure the children would cope with the reality of their father's death.

Harold planned a big vacation getaway so that the children could relax and have a little fun. They went to a resort for children in Orlando Florida. They stayed for a week. Harold suggested that Katrina and Alexis go shopping while he and TJ did a little shopping of their own. Harold and TJ were in the car and Harold said, "TJ, I love your mother very much. I love you and your sister too. I want to ask you something, and I want you to be very honest with me, okay."

"Okay," TJ said.

"Would you like for me to be a part of your lives permanently?"

"You mean like come and live with us?"

"Yes,"

"Yeah, that'll be cool, and you don't have to go home because you'll be right there with us like a daddy, huh?"

Harold smiled, "Yes, like a daddy. Would you like that?"

"I would like it. Me and my sister talk about it a lot. Lexi likes you. She says that she wished you were our daddy. I do too."

"Would it be alright with you if I asked your mother to marry me?" TJ got excited.

"That would make her so happy. I would be happy too. Momma likes you a lot. She says nice things about you and when we talk about you, she smiles. You make momma smile. My daddy made her cry all the time and he hurt her a lot. You're not like him. You take good care of her. I want you to be her husband."

"Thank you, son. I want to ask her to marry me. Would you like to go with me to a special place to buy her a nice ring?"

"Yes," TJ said.

He and Harold went to an appointment with a jeweler that Harold had already set up. He had flown him in just to meet with him in Florida because he'd planned on asking her. He and TJ picked out the most amazing ring. In all, Harold spent more than two hundred thousand on the ring. He also purchased a cute little diamond ring for Alexis as well as a watch for TJ. They went back to the resort, and they all went out to dinner. Harold caught Katrina off guard. "Katrina, I have something I want to ask you and Alexis. Now, I've already talked with my man TJ here, and he gave me permission to ask you two ladies this question. Katrina, I love you and Alexis, I love you and TJ. I want to be a permanent part of your lives." He presented the ring to her,

"Katrina darling; will you marry me?"

"Yes, Harold I'll marry you!" He placed the ring on her finger as she squealed with delight.

He turned his attention towards Alexis, took her right hand, and asked, "Alexis, I would love to be a father to you and take care of you as my own. I'll provide for you, your brother, and your mother. I'll give you the best life has to offer and the love you all deserve. Would you be my daughter?" He placed the ring that he had bought her on her little finger. She smiled and hugged Harold.

"This means you're going to be my new daddy!"

"TJ has already agreed," Harold said.

Katrina looked at TJ and, hugging him, said, "Come here you!"

It was a joyous occasion, and they were all excited. They gained the attention of the entire restaurant and everyone there congratulated the couple and celebrated with them. They enjoyed the rest of their vacation and afterwards flew home. Katrina couldn't wait to tell Chandra. She immediately got busy with wedding plans.

WEDDING DAY

Their big day had finally arrived and their family and friends were in attendance. There to be two ceremonies that day. Harold had the adoption papers drawn up to adopt TJ and Alexis, and he would be signing them that day along with the marriage license. The wedding began. Chandra was the maid-of-honor and Dale was Harold's best man. TJ walked his mother down the aisle, and they stood together as a family unit. The pastor performed the children's adoption ceremony first and then he performed the wedding. Harold had purchased gifts for the children with their new last names on them and he and Katrina presented them to the children as their new last names were being called out.

The family turned to the audience and the Pastor said, "Ladies and gentlemen, I present to you, "The

Sloane family!" Everyone was so moved by the ceremony that there wasn't a dry eye in the place. Everyone went to the reception, and it was a grand celebration. Afterwards, Harold and his new family left for their honeymoon vacation. Harold had set it up so his parents, Chandra, Dale, and Ms. Ruth could all go on their honeymoon vacation. Harold had flown an entire staff over with them to care for the children and to attend to their every need. He and Katrina were allowed plenty of alone time to enjoy their honeymoon in peace. They settled into their suite and ordered their dinner. While they waited for dinner to be served, they snuggled up close.

"Katrina sweetheart, you've made me the happiest man in the world. I'd been praying for years for a family and it appeared as though it would never happen for me. I was living prosperously in every area of my life, but I've always felt I was missing something. You were that missing part of me. The

Lord has answered my prayers by giving me a lovely wife and two wonderful children. I am profoundly grateful. I love you, baby."

"I love you too Harold. I'd been hoping for years that I would experience real love. For years I suffered harsh abuses at the hands of others, and I coped with it in silence. I prayed to God, and it seemed my prayers were not being heard, so I gave up. My only hope was my children. When I met you, I was drawn to you, but I was afraid. I wanted to run you off, but you wouldn't hear of it. I'm so grateful to God for everything he's done in my life. Look at how things have turned out. I'm on my honeymoon with the most amazing man in the world, the father of my children and my husband. I love you, Mr. Sloane," she said kissing him. "I love you too Mrs. Sloane." They skipped dinner and made love. Afterwards, Harold went to sleep. Katrina couldn't sleep so she went to the living-room quarters of the suite. She looked out of the window and saw a figure of an elderly woman. She walked over to the window for a closer look. The lady looked right at her and smiled. She resembled the lady who had given her the bible at the bus stop. Katrina asked herself *"Is that Mrs. Effie? It couldn't be. What would she be doing all the way over here?"* The lady reached into her purse and pulled out a bible. She smiled at Katrina, and she looked toward heaven. A wonderful, bright light shown around her. Katrina looked closely, fixing her eyes on her, but the lady was gone. "What in the world?" Katrina was puzzled. She went and got her bible and read it. She immediately opened it to Hebrews thirteen and read verse two. *"Don't forget to be kind and hospitable to people you don't know; they could be an angel, and you may not be aware of it.* She closed her bible and looked towards heaven, "Thank you, Father, and Mrs. Effie." She got into bed with Harold. He placed his arms around her and pulled her close, and they slept in the presence of Love.

A closing note from the author...

You never know what makes a good girl go bad...I have learned never to say what you will or won't do, especially if you've never lived in another person's shoes. Some people process trauma and grief differently, especially if help or resources are unavailable to them. Some may not understand the hurt and pain in others' lives and have judged them according to their actions, and not the underlying cause. Let's use our resources to assist others instead of judging them.

Some people have lived extremely traumatic lives and are able to overcome the obstacles and experience total victory. They may use their traumatic experiences to help others who have also lived traumatic lives. They have a hidden assignment from Father to minister to others. Jesus himself, who knew no sin, voluntarily came to earth, was ostracized and ridiculed by others, and was crucified to give His life for us because of His/Our Father's love.

There are various roads on the journey of life. Each of us must follow the road mapped out for us and not allow the opinions of others to dictate how we should carry out our duties designed by our Father and our heavenly hosts.

Jesus loved us so much that he was willing to suffer so that they all may be free.

ABOUT THE AUTHOR

Karen Coleman is an Arkansas native. She enjoys writing exciting and dramatic stories. A phenomenal author with a distinctive style, she has demonstrated a sensational talent for steering her readers through every line and page with eager anticipation.

Karen has published several novels in various genres. Readers have described her novels as riveting, fast-paced, and thrilling.

Her teen novels are insightful and empowering. As a mentor who has worked with teens for many years, Karen understands the social challenges they face, and she skillfully addresses those topics with a finesse that lends excitement, adventure, and encouragement.

A self-proclaimed writer of fiction with an element of truth, Karen began penning her thoughts as a hobby. After many years of writing and encouragement from those around her, she began writing on a more intense level, eventually turning out several wonderful novels. She offers something for almost every reader, from her adult crime series to her teen books, there's something to be enjoyed by all. Her literary works have garnered much fanfare and have not only been enjoyed by her many readers; she's highly celebrated among her writing peers. Her books are meant to inspire, uplift, and entertain leaving her audience asking for more.

Karen is also a playwright, actor, and former city council member. She's the mother of four and a Glam-ma of thirteen and counting. Her grandchildren affectionately call her Nana. She's also the proud mom of two rambunctious miniature schnauzers. When not writing or spoiling her grandbabies, she spends her time crafting, fishing, or enjoying a great barbecue.

OTHER BOOKS BY AUTHOR KAREN COLEMAN

CLOSER THAN ENEMIES 1

CLOSER THAN ENEMIES 2

ARKANSAS HEAT A CITY SCORNED

ARKANSAS HEAT A BRUTHA'S OBSESSION

ARKANSAS HEAT CINDY'S REVENGE

ARKANSAS HEAT DECEPTIVE PRACTICE

ARKANSAS HEAT RAISING DELGADO

WHATEVER HAPPENED TO I LOVE YOU?

NO PLACE FOR EMILY ANN

EMILY ANN & FRIENDS COLORING BOOK

MORGAN'S PATH

IN THE WRONG GAME

FROZEN DREAMS

METAMORPHOSIS: GOOD GIRL GONE BAD

I AM A WHOLE BEING; FINDING WHOLENESS AFTER REJECTION, ABANDONMENT, PAIN, AND LOSS

I AM A WHOLE BEING JOURNALS AND WORKBOOKS FOR ADULTS AND TEENS.